CW00728479

CATCH TH

CATCH THE MOON

Sue Welford

MACMILLAN CHILDREN'S BOOKS

First published1989 by
MACMILLAN CHILDREN'S BOOKS
A division of Macmillan Publishers Limited
London and Basingstoke
Associated companies throughout the world

Paperback edition published 1990

British Library Cataloguing in Publication Data
Welford, Sue
Catch the moon.
I. Title II. Series
813'.914[F]

ISBN 0-333-48481-9

Printed in Hong Kong

For
Melissa and Adam
and
Lynnet

CATCH THE MOON

This morning I made a decision. I decided to write about Stephen. For a long time now I seem to have been living in a glass pyramid – separated, yet looking out. The world is living: I am no part of it. This morning I decided it was about time I escaped.

I woke early and looked out of the window. The roof of the summerhouse was just visible through the trees. The birds were singing. There was that blue–grey haze over everything that you know heralds a hot day. Beyond the trees I could see the meadow. An early-morning lark rose in the air. The top of the church tower stuck out above the mist like an emerging ghost. There is something reassuring about that tower. Through it all, through the earthquake that shook our lives, that tower was always there.

This house used to be the vicarage, a long time ago before my father's family owned it. There was once a path from the garden across the stream and through the meadow to the church beyond. Village folk walked it every Sunday. Twice a day, sometimes three, and at midnight on Christmas Eve. I wonder if it really did always snow on those olden-day Christmas Eves? It never does now.

The house is solid and square and grey. It abounds with simplicity. Its only concession to ornamentation is a gargoyle in each corner. Even the yellow rose that climbs up one wall seems to be intruding.

In the roof are tiny bedrooms where servant-girls slept. These rooms are full of junk now. Relics from the family who had the house as their country home. There is a narrow staircase leading from the kitchen. I try to imagine those poor girls. Crawling out of bed on bitter winter mornings – the water in the wash-jugs frozen solid. I bet they hoped for summer. Hoped endlessly for days such as this. Days that remind me of that glorious summer I spent with Stephen.

Chapter One

We were all there when my father dropped the bombshell. Blun (short for Mrs Blundell. Her name's Daisy but we never call her that), who helps look after the house. I love her dearly. She's been like a mother to me all the years since my real one died. I talk to her a lot but there are things even she doesn't understand.

My Aunt Jo was there too. She lives with us. She's a bit batty but I'll tell you about her in a minute. My father was there, and me of course. We were all sitting round the breakfast table – except Blun. She was washing up.

'Rina – I have something to tell you,' my father said. He had finished his toast. I knew he had something on his mind. He seemed nervous. Folding and unfolding the newspaper, never really reading it. He cleared his throat.

Aunt Jo looked over the top of her spectacles at him. She wore a pair of those round, steel-rimmed ones like John Lennon used to wear. She looked like a small-eyed nervous owl. The wide sleeve of her dress had dragged in the marmalade but she didn't seem to notice. She never noticed anything, my Aunt Jo. She lived in a kind of fantasy world.

1

She painted a lot, landscapes mostly. She went to jumble sales and bought long dresses. Sometimes she wore two, one on top of the other because she couldn't decide which one to put on. Her greatest love was wild creatures, squirrels, birds. In fact she made cakes for them. Gooey messes of melted fat, nuts and currants. She was really crazy but I loved her.

'Rina!' I looked up from my book, brushing off toast crumbs that had fallen between the pages.

'Did you hear me? I've got something to tell you.'

'What?'

'Well, put your book down for a minute.'

I put it down reluctantly. Breakfast was usually a non-speaking experience in our house. I was relying on it at the moment to cram in a bit of last-minute revising. I looked at my father expectantly, wishing he would get on with it. He still seemed to be having difficulty finding the right words.

'Rina,' he blurted out at last, 'I'm getting married.'

'Getting *married*!'

Surely I'd heard him wrong? Surely he wouldn't announce such a thing casually at the breakfast table? Surely there must be special occasions put aside to announce things like that?

Aunt Jo looked at me again, frowning, sucking her lips noisily. I wished she'd put her teeth in before breakfast. I knew she was trying to gauge my reaction.

'Yes,' my father said calmly.

'Who on earth to?' I almost shouted.

'To Jean Grey – she came down for the New Year. Don't you remember her?'

I thought back. My father often brought friends to the house. Business people mostly. Something to do with publishing like himself. I don't know exactly what he did do but whatever it was you had to be clever to do it. When his friends came Blun would come over and cook special meals. As I got older I was allowed to eat with them. Generally their conversation was stuffy and boring. I knew my father expected me to take over the role of cook when I was old enough.

Maybe when he got married to this Jean Grey person then she'd do it instead. I had already told my father that just because I was a girl it didn't mean I had to like cooking. Actually I had been old enough to do the cooking for ages but had so far avoided the trap.

But Jean Grey . . . I *did* remember her. My father had some business colleagues visit us for Christmas – she was among them and had stayed on for a couple of days afterwards. I remember she was small and blonde – a very neat Grey person. I hadn't had much to do with her but I remember my father seemed happy when she was here. Acting the fool, cracking jokes – not like him at all. I must have been blind not to see what was going on. But why hadn't he told me about her before? I always knew he must have women friends – I didn't suppose he had never had any relationships with women since my mother died. He wasn't a monk or anything. But

3

as he'd never brought them home I'd never thought about it much.

'But why didn't you tell me about her?' I asked. He shrugged and looked worried.

'I don't really know, Rina. I suppose I wanted to be sure of my feelings – to be sure she'd have me before I committed myself. *And* I didn't know how you'd react.'

'Will it make any difference *how* I react?'

I could feel my face going red. How *could* he think about marrying anybody, bringing a stranger to the house? God, I'd even do the cooking if I thought it would make him change his mind. A suspicious prickling behind my eyes told me I'd have to leave the table or else I'd cry. I'd probably cry anyway but at least no one would see. I hated that, people seeing me cry – especially my father.

Aunt Jo watched. Gauging me.

'Well, I would like you to be pleased,' my father said. He threw a glance at Blun. She watched me too. Watched my reaction. There was a deathly pause.

I swallowed noisily. 'I don't see why you want to get married,' I said, managing to control my voice and making it sound *almost* normal. 'Aren't we all right as we are – haven't we managed all right since Mummy died?'

My father sighed. 'Yes, Rina, we have. And you know I loved your mother and missed her dreadfully but she has been dead for ten years – I *need* another wife, Rina.' He threw Blun another despairing glance as if he knew he was making a

4

hash of the whole thing. Only he wasn't – it was me who was making a hash of things.

'You haven't before,' I said before I could stop myself. Feeling the anger rising. Feeling the pain.

My father's face took on that resolute look that meant this time he was determined to win. I knew that nothing I could say would make him change his mind. I looked down at my plate.

'Rina,' my aunt piped up. 'Look at your father when he's talking to you.'

'Shut up, Aunt Jo,' I said through my teeth. Why did she have to butt in? This was something between my father and me.

But I did look at him again. My face was flaming and I knew it. I just wanted to get out. To run.

My father's look of resolution changed to one of anxiety. What I really wanted was to throw my arms around him and beg him not to marry this Grey person. But my father wasn't the kind of man you could do that to. Displays of affection embarrassed him. I suppose it was some hang-up from his childhood. When I was small I used to long for him to cuddle me but he never did. I remember my mother cuddling me. But then she died. My father used to hold my hand, though, when he took me out for walks. I used to think that must be what heaven was like. Walking along, a strong hand holding yours. I wondered if he held the Grey person's hand. I wondered if *she* thought it was heaven.

I stood up abruptly. My book fell to the floor.

'Rina!'

My father put out a hand to stop me walking past.

'I've got nothing more to say,' I yelled, dodging past and running out. I ran upstairs. I threw myself on my bed. My tears wet the pillow. I picked up my poor old Bear and threw him across the room. He lay in a corner. Face down. Limbs twisted.

The door opened.

Blun. Face like thunder. 'Rina, get up!'

I sat up and sniffed. I wiped my nose on the sleeve of my sweatshirt.

'I'm ashamed of you.'

I was ashamed of myself.

I wouldn't look at her. She sat beside me and held my arms, shaking me.

'Now stop behaving like a spoilt child – how can you be so selfish?'

'It's him that's being selfish,' I said bitterly, turning away. Even as the words came out I knew how stupid I was being. Sometimes it's like that – you know you're being silly but the tide of anger just sweeps you along with it. There's no escape. No turning back.

Blun pushed the hair away from my face. She tucked some behind my ears. She used to do that when I was little. Close to her I noticed she was beginning to look really old. Hair grey. Skin wrinkled. Hard work all her life had reddened her hands, the joints knobbly with arthritis. I loved her so much. I began to cry again. She held me close, comforting, rocking me to and fro. I was bigger than her but she held me just the same.

6

'Don't cry, lovey – it'll be all right. Just you wait and see.' Her voice had a West Country twang. It reminded me of apples and warm blankets.

She held me away from her and took a tissue to wipe my eyes. She looked at me, frowning a bit.

'You know your father does *need* another kind of relationship. His marriage to Mrs Grey will make him very happy.'

'But why isn't he happy now?' I felt betrayed that my father needed someone else.

'He *is* happy, Rina, but he has been lonely. I've seen it in his face, in his manner. Don't spoil things for him – he cares about you so much.'

'If he cared for me he wouldn't be bringing a stranger to the house.'

'That's rubbish, and you know it.'

I hung my head. Knowing it.

'Now promise me you'll at least try.' She squeezed my arms. Even though I was well past my sixteenth birthday Blun always made me feel like a little girl.

'But . . . '

'Promise me, Rina!'

I sniffed. 'Okay. I'll try.'

She kissed me. She hugged me. Over her shoulder I saw my father standing in the doorway. He had come up the stairs silently – footsteps drowned by my selfishness. Blun smoothed my hair, then went out. My father came and took her place.

'I'm sorry, Daddy,' I said, looking down at my hands clasped together in my lap. I wanted to hug him, too.

'It's all right, Rina – I should have found a better way to tell you.' To my surprise he took my hands in his. They were huge. One almost covered both of mine.

'It's really my fault,' he went on. 'I should have prepared you, brought her here again to get to know you. It's just that she has a business in London, a dress shop – a boutique I think you'd call it – and she finds it hard to get away.'

I sniffed but didn't say anything. I thought I'd just let him rattle on and I'd learn more about the Grey person without actually having to ask.

'You know I love you, don't you, Rina?'

I nodded. Knowing it but wishing he'd say it more often.

'And you know you've been a great comfort to me since Mummy died?'

I nodded again.

'It's just that I need another kind of relationship, Rina, and one that's *permanent*, can you understand that?'

I nodded again. I began to feel like Andy Pandy or someone, nodding like a twit.

'Of course,' I said, deciding it was about time I said something. 'I'm not a kid.' I was trying desperately at that moment not to think about my father in bed with the Grey person. In bed with anyone.

'Then promise me you'll try and get on with her. I know it won't be easy for you. It won't be easy for her either. Promise me you'll try, Rina?'

'Will she be here all the time?' I had visions of her trying to run my life.

'Well, she'll live here, of course.'

'No – I mean will she still have the shop – go up to London every day like you?'

'She's going to get a manager, but she'll still go up several times a week.'

I heaved a silent sigh of relief. At least she wouldn't be here all the time, trying to interfere with what I did. But I still couldn't really see why she had to be here at all. Not as my father's wife anyway.

'But Daddy,' I said, 'do you actually have to *marry* her – I mean can't she just come and live here – it would be much more sensible, then if you got fed up with her . . . '

My father interrupted. 'Rina, I want to marry her. And she wants to marry me. We are both old-fashioned enough to believe that if you love someone you should marry them . . . Rina . . . ?' He squeezed my hands. 'I missed your mother *so* much when she died – I've had other women friends of course but no one I wanted to marry. I had you and Jo and we were a proper family . . . ' he broke off. I saw fear in his eyes, fear of growing old, alone. 'But you'll be off making your own life in a year or so. Who will keep me company then?'

'Aunt Jo?'

My father smiled. A weary smile, as though the fight with me had exhausted him. I smiled back. Suddenly I knew that everything would be okay. I *had* to make it okay whether I liked it or not. And I'd have to try to like the wretched Grey person too – for my father's sake.

'. . . and now I'll have Jean as well,' he said.

We smiled together, sharing secrets.

And then he told me about Stephen.

Chapter Two

I remember the first day I met him – Stephen, I mean. I was sitting by the stream that runs along the end of the garden. It's my favourite place. I often take my sketchbook down there. Sometimes I write poems. There're sticklebacks and kingfishers and great, golden king-cups – all sorts of things to sit quietly and watch.

That day I was just thinking. I do a lot of that. It's funny how you can get your thoughts together just by sitting quietly in a quiet place. Only the sound of water for company, the whisper of wind through grasses. I loved it there at night too. The dark sounds of small animals, the cry of an owl. They made me shiver. Sometimes when the water is low and lies still in shallow, thoughtful pools, you can see the reflection of the moon. When I was small I'd dream I could scoop it up in my hands – hold it there – make a wish. I knew exactly what I'd have wished that day if I had the moon in my hands. I'd have wished he'd never come, this strange youth, this mysterious son of my stepmother.

Actually I reckoned I'd been very good. My father and Jean had got married in London – some register office or other. We hadn't gone to the wedding, any of us. I think my father thought I wouldn't want to. I think he was afraid Aunt Jo might show him up. Turning up in one of her crazy jumble dresses. It would have been a laugh if she had.

We had welcomed Jean to the house, though. Jo and Blun and me. We had stood on the doorstep when they arrived. Like a delegation. Jean had kissed me and admired my hair. No one had ever done *that* before. She had looked at me questioningly but I had no answers to give her. Against my better judgement I smiled at her. She was smaller than me – only about five feet. My father looked like a giant beside her. My mother had been small too. Maybe he liked small women. I didn't say anything to Jean. Just smiled. It seemed to be enough. I suppose my father had warned her about me.

She had kissed Aunt Jo too, knocking her hat askew. I giggled. Blun frowned.

I had wondered if the beloved son would arrive with them, but we had to wait for that pleasure. Apparently he went to some private school or other and their term ended before ours so he would be here soon. I just knew what he'd be like. Snobby and arrogant – all the things you think private schoolboys are going to be.

'I do hope you'll be friends,' my father had said. I suppose he thought I'd been lonely all these years, too. I suppose he thought I'd missed having brothers and sisters. I hadn't. I liked being on my own. I was like my mother, Blun said. She had liked her own company too. She was red-haired, like me. Quick to anger. Quick to love. I remember her shouting at me, then swinging me up in her arms, hugging me to make up. I was six when she died. Sometimes I try to imagine what it would be like if she was still alive. I wondered if I'd fight with her like most girls do. It was hard to imagine, though, having a mother. It was something other people had – not me. I'd got used to it.

'I hope he won't interfere with my stuff,' I had said selfishly. I'm ashamed now how selfish I was. I suppose it came from never having to share anything with anyone. And being afraid. Afraid someone would take away the things I loved.

'Of course he won't, dear,' Jean had said patiently. Her everlasting patience was beginning to get on my nerves. I wasn't used to people being patient with me. Only Blun, of course, and she was different. Jean wanted to be my friend so much she was trying too hard.

A week later the beloved son arrived.

Jean had been in a tizz all week. She hadn't been to work once – spending hours on the phone but never setting foot outside the house. She had been putting the finishing touches to Stephen's newly decorated bedroom. She'd looked at her watch that day at least every five minutes. She even went off to the station an hour before the train was due and it was only fifteen minutes' drive away. If she loved him so much I wondered why she had sent him away in the first place.

While she was gone I sat in the kitchen helping Blun make some sandwiches for tea. The kitchen was a lot tidier since Jean arrived. You could actually find things. Blun did her best but Jo and I weren't very good at putting things away.

'What do you think Stephen'll be like, Blun?' I asked. As well as being arrogant I had imagined him treating me like some inferior being – a kid even. I needed reassurance.

'Very nice, dear, I expect – public schoolboys always are.'

'Pooh,' I snorted, 'they're not, you know. I'm always reading in the paper about them getting expelled for smoking pot and having girls in their rooms and stuff like that.'

'Well, that just shows they're normal, healthy boys.'

'What, smoking pot . . . ?' I hooted, cracking up. 'Oh Blun, you are funny.'

'Well, not that,' she said hurriedly, 'you know very well what I mean. I'm sure you'll find he's very nice.'

Oh yes, I thought bitterly, I'm sure he'll be very *nice* – poncing about the place like a lord.

'Anyway,' Blun went on, 'his mother's a very pleasant woman and there's no reason why he shouldn't be very pleasant too.'

She gave me one of her piercing looks. I grinned. Dear old Blun. She could always manage to get right to the secret core of my thoughts.

14

'People aren't always like their parents,' I observed. 'Why do people always think we have to be, why can't we just be ourselves?'

I piled a stack of sandwiches on to a plate, poking back the bits of cucumber that had fallen out. 'Surely that'll be enough? We haven't got the whole village coming to tea have we?'

'If young Stephen eats anything like my lads did at that age we'll need more than that.'

A picture flashed into my mind. Not only would he be stuck-up and arrogant. He would also be *fat*!

'He's not young,' I blurted out, determined to hate him for something, even if it was only his age. 'He's seventeen – almost eighteen.'

'Well, that's hardly old.' Blun smiled, looking at me again.

I got up and hugged her.

'Are you going to change?' she asked.

I looked down at my tatty old jeans. 'Why?'

'I just thought you might.'

I leaned my elbow on her shoulder. 'I might,' I said, grinning.

She slapped my bottom and told me to go away.

I went to my room and put on my favourite Rod Stewart tape. I took off my jeans and sweatshirt and stood in front of the mirror in my pants. I turned sideways. This way, then that. I was definitely too skinny. Hardly any breasts, slim hips like a boy. Although I was red-haired my skin wasn't freckly, thank God. I put my hands over my breasts. They began to tingle. I thought about my father in bed

15

with the Grey person. I tried to imagine his hands on her breasts, covering them. Making love. It didn't seem right. I don't know why.

I gathered my hair on top of my head. Wisps fell down. They always do when you've got hair as thick as mine. I pirouetted again. With my hair up I looked older. I let it go. At the front it covered my breasts. I wished they were bigger.

I lay down on the bed. On the wall, among the posters, was a drawing I'd done of my father. Even though I say it myself, it was quite good. Because it was charcoal his hair could have been fair instead of grey. The shadows had erased some of the lines around his eyes. He'd looked better, happier, since his marriage, and I was glad.

I thought of Aunt Jo. Doubtless sitting in the garden somewhere in front of her easel. Oblivious to everything. Oblivious to the fact that the beloved son was due to arrive and might change our lives for ever. I bet she had one of her long dresses on. Draped around her like a butterfly's wing. I wondered if I'd ever be like her, dreaming my life away. Dreaming of the past. Dreaming of a lover killed in the war. Of parents killed by bombs.

I was still lying there enjoying the soft feel of the quilt against my bare skin when I heard Jean's car coming up the drive. Our drive is gravelly and you can hear cars long before they come round the corner.

I pulled on my yellow dungarees and an old Snoopy T-shirt and dived down the back stairs.

16

I couldn't face another reception committee. They could jolly well call me when they wanted me to meet this great and wonderful Stephen Grey.

But they didn't call me. Of all things they sent him to find me.

Chapter Three

It was really hot that June day. I was dangling my feet in the stream and wishing I'd tied my hair back from my face after all. The nape of my neck was sweating like anything. I put my head down and pulled my hair over as if I was going to wash it in the stream. I cupped a handful of water and splashed it on the back of my neck. It felt wonderfully sharp and refreshing. I wished the water was deep enough for me to swim. Naked. Cool.

I tossed my hair back then realised someone was standing behind me. Funny, I hadn't seen a reflection in the water. Maybe the someone was like Dracula and didn't have one.

I squinted up, tucking my hair behind my ear. I couldn't see properly. The sun made a kind of bright aura round the figure as if it was El Cid or something. I squeezed my eyelids together. Perhaps when I opened them it would be gone.

But it wasn't. He squatted down beside me.

Of course, I knew all the time who it was.

He had his mother's fair hair, high cheekbones. His skin was tanned as though he spent a lot of

18

time in the open air. I was surprised at that. I thought he'd have some kind of pallor – like prisoners get when they are locked up for a long time. His eyes were startlingly blue. His hair was quite long and lay on the nape of his neck softly as if it was caressing his skin. I could see he needed a shave.

'I'm Stephen,' he said unnecessarily.'They sent me to find you.'

It was strange, the feeling that came over me then. I had really been dreading meeting him. He had sounded so perfect when Jean had spoken of him. Perfect scholar, perfect son – ugh! Yet here he was squatting beside me, smiling, looking like a beautiful Greek god and here was I desperately searching for something incredibly nasty to say to him.

He wasn't dressed in school uniform as I'd im-agined. You know, pressed grey trousers, stuffy blazer with some sort of badge or other on, a tie. Instead he had ratty old plimsolls and jeans and a grubby T-shirt like me and my heart beat so loudly it seemed as if he might hear.

I bit the inside of my cheek and looked sideways at him.

'What do they want me for?' My hand plucked at the grass and I hoped to God he wouldn't see that it trembled.

He shrugged. 'Tea's ready, I suppose.'

He didn't even talk like an upper-class twit.

I felt myself growing annoyed. Why couldn't he have been hateful? Why couldn't he at least have acne? Every other boy in the world his age had at least one spot on his face.

'Has Blun put the food in the garden?' I asked shortly.

He frowned. 'Blun?'

'Yes, Blun,' I said impatiently, raising my eyes to the tree tops. God, didn't he even know who Blun was?

'Oh . . . you mean Mrs Blundell, the old lady helping my mother in the kitchen?'

'She's not *that* old!'

'Well . . . ' he coloured a bit, 'you know what I mean. Anyway, someone's put the food out on the garden table, I don't know who it was.'

He stood up and took a step back as if he didn't like being so near to me. As if I had BO or something.

'Well, I don't want any.'

I stood up too. I'm tall for my age but he was a lot taller. 'I hate bloody picnics,' I said, kicking at the turf. 'Tell them I'm not hungry.' I don't know what made me lie like that.

I looked at him defiantly and saw he was grinning.

'What's funny?' I snapped, hating him for being so gorgeous.

'Nothing.' He flushed again and looked away.

Suddenly I couldn't bear the thought of sitting with them all, eating cucumber sandwiches, making small talk as if it was some Victorian tea party. I mean, *really* couldn't bear it. I suppose I'd said that about hating picnics just so he'd know I wasn't particularly anxious to sit and eat with him but suddenly my whole appetite really did disappear and I'd been starving up till then.

'Aren't you coming then?'

'Does it look like it?'

I sat down again, my back towards him.

'Okay,' he said, uncaring.

When I looked round he'd gone.

Chapter Four

I sat there a while wondering what Stephen had thought of me. Spoilt brat, I expect. After all that was exactly how I was behaving. I wondered why he hadn't got angry and told me to tell them myself that I didn't want any tea. That's what I'd have done to someone as rude as me. If he had been sarcastic or arrogant it wouldn't have been so bad. He was just as Blun said. *Nice!*

Eventually I got up. I knew if I skirted the lawn, hiding behind the shrubbery, I could spy on them – see what they were up to. I used to do that when I was small – spy on my father talking to his friends, showing them the garden. I hadn't done it for years.

Sure enough there they were. The Grey person and my father sitting in deckchairs. Stephen stretched out on the grass. I could see him clearly – leaning on one elbow looking up at his mother as she spoke to him. I noticed for the first time that his jeans were very tight. Very sexy. He'd taken off his T-shirt. The sun shone on his skin. His hair fell over one eye and I saw him flick it back before he took a bite of his sandwich. I suddenly felt peculiar. I suppose it must have been hunger. I cursed myself for being so stupid.

I crept round to the kitchen and went in. Blun was getting ready to go home.

'Finished already?' she asked.

'I wasn't hungry,' I lied. I sat down at the kitchen table. I felt miserable.

'That's not like you – do you feel all right?'

'Fine,' I lied again. I fiddled with an apple from the fruit bowl, polishing it on my thigh.

'Did you meet Stephen?'

'Yes – thank you.'

'Well?' Blun put her apron in the drawer. I got up.

'Well nothing,' I said angrily. I knew she was watching me as I stormed out. Sometimes you can't even talk to the people you love most.

I didn't see much of him after that. I had two more exams to take and spent my time revising like mad. I saw him at dinner when I got back from school and that was about all. My father has this crazy idea that we should all sit down together for dinner each evening. I told him that no one did that any more. I said people just sat around the TV with their food on their laps. He wouldn't hear of us doing that.

'Preserving the last bastion of family life,' he said. That made me laugh although, deep down, I believed he was right.

Stephen didn't say much to me. I was glad. I didn't have anything to say to him either. Sometimes I watched him from under my eyelids as he ate his meal. His manners were sickeningly perfect. Passing the salt, passing the bread without even having to be asked. He talked to my father a lot. About cricket, about cars. Jean watched them both with adoring eyes. I felt left out. It was my own fault.

When Stephen had been home a few days a big trunk arrived from the station. All his things were in it. I passed his room. The door was open and I saw him putting some silver cups on his shelf. I stayed a while, leaning against the door frame, watching. He took some rolled-up posters from the trunk. Then he saw me so I ran to my room and banged the door.

'Rina!'

I heard him call but pretended I hadn't. It was crazy – I really wanted to speak to him, wanted to ask what the cups were for, what the posters were of but it was so hard. I already seemed to have built a wall between us that was impossible to break down.

He came and tapped on my door.

'What?' I didn't *mean* to sound irritated, it just came out like that.

'I wondered if you'd give me a hand?'

I opened the door. Just a bit. Just enough to see him standing there. He held some rolled-up posters.

'To do what?'

'Put up these – got any Blu-Tack?'

'There's some in the kitchen.'

'Will you help?'

I knew he could do it by himself quite easily – he was trying to be friends.

'I'm busy,' I said sharply. Then, feeling guilty, 'I've got some maths to do, it's my exam tomorrow.'

'Okay,' he shrugged. 'I . . . ' he paused, uncertain.

'What?' I said impatiently.

'I could help you if you like.'

'It's okay, I can manage.'

I shut the door in his face. I stood with my back against it, breathing hard. I heard him run down the stairs. I'd noticed he always ran everywhere. Then up again. He slammed his door.

It was strange. I couldn't concentrate on my maths at all. I cursed the wretched Stephen for putting me off. I put on a tape but even old Rod couldn't help me concentrate. I gazed out of the window – hating to be indoors on such a lovely day. I decided I would take my books and go and sit outside.

As I came out of my bedroom I heard a crash, then a thud. It came from Stephen's room. Then silence. My heart began to beat wildly – I listened. Nothing. I dropped my books, ran to his door and threw it open. He was sitting on the floor rubbing his elbow. He looked up at me ruefully. His hair fell over one eye.

'Broke the bloody chair,' he said.

I giggled then. I couldn't help it. He looked so funny. It's awful how you laugh when someone hurts themselves. *And* he'd busted one of my father's antique chairs. He'd be furious if he found out. That seemed the funniest thing of all.

Stephen looked at me for a minute then he

began to grin. Then he laughed too and struggled to his feet.

'Have you hurt yourself?' I asked.

'No – the chair doesn't look too good, though.'

I went in, still grinning.

'Never mind – I'll put it up in one of the attic rooms – no one'll ever notice.' I picked up the bits. He made a move to help me. I stepped back quickly. He picked up the broken leg and handed it to me.

'Can you manage?'

'I'm not weak.'

'I know that.' We looked at each other. For the first time I noticed he had a few freckles on his nose. 'Thanks,' he said.

I turned and left him. I knew he was watching as I went along the landing. At the bottom of the attic stairs I turned and said – 'Get yourself another one from the spare room.'

'Okay, thanks.'

The poster he had been putting up was one of Marilyn Monroe.

At dinner that evening I asked in a whisper if he had found another chair. He grinned and whispered he had.

'Does Marilyn Monroe always make you lose your balance?' I said.

'Not always.'

The Grey person was looking at us so I didn't speak to him again.

The maths exam was awful – the final one. At last I was free.

* * *

The next day I found Stephen down by the stream. I thought I'd be annoyed seeing him sitting in my place. I wasn't. When I approached he jumped up.

'Sorry.'

'What for?'

'Sitting in your place.'

I shrugged. 'It's okay – you're not stopping me.'

I sat down with my back to him. 'How do you know I come down here anyway.'

'I've seen you.'

'Have you been spying on me?'

'No, of course not – why should I do a thing like that? I saw you that first day. Anyway, what makes you think I'm interested in what you do?' He sounded defensive, angry.

I shrugged. 'Nothing really.'

I was about to say something else but when I turned round he'd gone. I bit my lip. Then, on impulse, I got up and ran after him. I found him standing in front of the summerhouse – hands in pockets. He must have heard me coming because he said, without turning, 'What's in there?'

'Just junk.' I was surprised he could sound so relaxed when a minute ago he had been angry. If I'm angry I stay that way for hours.

'What kind of junk?' He put his face to the glass and peered in. He rubbed the window pane with his finger but the dirt was on the inside as well as outside.

'Just rubbish, an old settee, a few ratty old tennis rackets.'

'I'd like to see inside,' – he turned – 'if I may.'

'Do what you like,' I said. 'This is supposed to be your home too, isn't it?'

'Is it?' he said, still looking at me. I knew then that my answer would make all the difference in the world to him. I could tell by the look in his eyes. I could always tell what Stephen was thinking by the look in his eyes.

'Yes,' I said.

He grinned. Slowly. His eyes twinkled at me. We stood there like two stupid fools grinning at each other and I knew that he had been just as scared and apprehensive as me about coming to live here. And all the time the birds sang as if nothing spectacular had just happened. The breeze rustled the bushes. Mr Blun had cut the lawn that morning and I could smell that gorgeous smell of cut grass mixed with the sweet scent of the old rambler rose that hugged the summerhouse.

Even now, smelling those smells reminds me of that summer I spent with Stephen.

Chapter Five

'Have you done all your exams?' Stephen asked when we had finished looking in the summerhouse.

I made a face. 'Yes – thank God.' I knew he was doing four A-levels and probably thought exams were easy.

'Will you have to go back to school to finish the term?'

'We're supposed to but I shan't,' I said. 'There's lots of things I want to do at home.'

'Like what?'

'I'm going to repair the old boat for a start.'

I had wanted to do it for ages but had been too busy studying.

'What for?'

'So I can take it down to the creek, stupid. We used to have great fun with it when I was small.'

'I'll help you if you like.'

I shrugged. 'If you want,' I said indifferently.

In spite of everything I was still trying to hate him.

It was while we were repairing the boat that I really got to know Stephen. I found out he wasn't at all like some boys I knew. He didn't tease me

29

about my hair, or try to get his hand up my skirt. Lots of my ideas he agreed with. About the bomb, animal rights, women's lib – that kind of thing. *And* he liked Rod Stewart. Best of all he talked to me as an equal, not as if I were only some simpering twit of a girl who might be interesting in bed but nowhere else. He thought women could do anything men could, and should have the opportunity to try.

Best of all he made me feel that my ideas were really important and interesting and he listened, I mean *really* listened to what I'd got to say.

I listened to him, too. He told me what he thought about things. About his hopes and dreams.

Mostly I was curious about his school and what sort of things they got up to there. I asked him.

'It's all right,' he said, sitting cross-legged painting the opposite side of the boat. He grinned at me from over the gunwale. I always had a faint suspicion that maybe he was teasing me but managing to disguise it so I didn't really know whether he was or not.

'What do you mean – all right?' I said impatiently. 'Don't you hate being shut up there nine months of the year?'

He laughed. 'We're not shut up – anyway I've never known anything else.'

'Have you always been at boarding school?'

'Since I was seven.'

I felt a stab of pity. 'Were you an awful child then – is that why you were sent away?'

He laughed again. He had a wide mouth and

30

strong, even teeth. I hated it when he laughed at me although I knew he wasn't being nasty. That's why I went on making friends instead of ignoring him, I suppose.

'I wasn't *sent* away,' he said, 'my mother had the shop to run and she thought I'd be better off with people of my own age, that's all.'

'What about your father?'

A kind of shutter came down over his face when I said that. It was curious – one minute his face was alive and smiling. The next cold, hard, uncaring. He looked down, swiping away furiously with the paint brush.

'I never knew him,' he said. There was great bitterness in his voice.

'How come?'

'I just never knew him, that's all. He left before I was born.'

'Left where?'

'My mother – well, they weren't actually married but he left her – went away.'

'And she had to look after you all on her own?'

'That's right.'

'Why? Why did he leave, was he married to someone else?'

Stephen shrugged – I could see he didn't want to talk about it but I was determined to find out some more.

'I don't know,' he said.

'Where is he now?'

Stephen shrugged again. 'Dead for all I care,' he said.

'He must have been a real rat.'

'Yes.'

'You must wonder about him – what he looked like, what kind of person he was.'

'I used to when I was young – it doesn't bother me now.' By the way Stephen looked, it bothered him a lot.

'Why don't you ask your mother?'

'I did, several times, but she wouldn't tell me. Said it was all in the past and was best forgotten.'

'That's daft – you've got a right to know.'

'Well, I don't want to know, not any more. For God's sake, Rina, let's talk about something else.'

'Well,' I said, wanting the last word as usual, 'if he went off like that then he's not worth knowing about anyway. And if he *is* dead that makes you half an orphan like me.'

Stephen smiled. One of those dazzling smiles I would come to know so well.

'That's right,' he said. 'Another thing we've got in common.'

Not for the first time I wished he wasn't so flipping nice. I felt sorry for him, for Jean too, being abandoned like that. Lots of women bring up kids on their own now but in those days it must have been really hard. In spite of myself I felt some admiration for Jean. At least my mother couldn't help dying and leaving my father on his own. I didn't at all like feeling sorry for her, or Stephen for that matter. In fact I wished desperately there was something I could hate him for but there was nothing – not one single thing.

'Didn't your mother ever meet anyone else?' I asked, still curious. 'Until my father, that is?'

'I don't really know,' Stephen said. 'I suppose she must have had men friends but I never saw any of them. She never brought anyone to visit me at school. She's always been so independent – never seemed to need anyone.'

'Only you.'

He grinned ruefully. 'Only me,' he said.

'Didn't you ever mind being . . . illegitimate?'

He laughed. 'A bastard you mean.'

'Well . . . ' I hated that word, it sounded horrible.

'No – I didn't mind. It was better than having parents who fight all the time like some of my friends.'

'Yes, I suppose it must be.' I knew people too whose parents didn't get along. They came to school with awful tales of rows and hysterics – fights even, sometimes. Real fights. I would hate that too. I found myself liking Stephen more and more. I just couldn't help it. We had so much in common it was inevitable we should be friends.

After we'd finished the boat and put it out on the drive to dry we decided to go for a walk.

We came across Aunt Jo with her easel.

'It's nice to see you two getting along so well,' she said as we stopped to look at her picture. I stuck my tongue out at Stephen above her head. He grinned. Jo put down her palette. The hem of her floral dress touched the grass. She wore a wide straw hat with a load of artificial flowers pinned to the brim. A bee hovered expectantly. Aunt Jo flapped her skinny hands around her head.

'Shoo,' she said, 'shoo.'

'It won't hurt you if you keep still,' Stephen said politely.

Now if I'd have said something like that she would have told me off but sweetness and honey dripped from his tongue and she took it like a lamb. I suppose that was one thing they taught you at boarding school – how to be rude in the politest possible way.

I made another face at him. I could see he was trying to suppress a grin. He bent over my aunt solicitously.

'That's awfully good,' he said.

She smiled up at him, fluttering her scant eyelashes like a young girl.

'Why, thank you, Stephen.' She sounded genuinely surprised. Actually the picture *was* good – I had to admit it. I was always on at her to exhibit her stuff in the village hall but she never would. She seemed to have no wish to share her talents with other people. She just stacked her pictures away with all the others in her bedroom and forgot about them.

'Come on,' I said, tugging Stephen's arm. 'See you later, Aunt Jo.'

Stephen gave her another of his dazzling smiles. He allowed me to drag him away. Out of hearing distance we burst into helpless giggles.

'Do you always charm old ladies?' I asked between snorts.

'Usually,' he said.

I looked at him. I tried to detect some kind of arrogance in his look or in his tone of voice. There wasn't any.

We walked along in silence for a bit. The sun beat down like hot irons pressed to our heads. Walking along our hands almost touched.

'You know,' Stephen said suddenly as if he had been thinking about saying it for a long time and had only just plucked up the courage. 'I dreaded meeting you. I thought you'd hate me coming to live with you.'

'Why?' I said, wondering if he had been able to read my thoughts that first day by the stream.

'Well, John' – John's my father – 'said you weren't like other girls. He said you had a fiery temper. He thought you might resent having to share things.'

I stopped to pick a blade of grass and when I stood up he was staring at me. He put out his hand and touched my hair. You know, one of those silly bits that stick out all the time.

'Do you?' he asked softly.

I jerked my head away. 'Do I what?'

'Mind me being here?'

Without really meaning to I said, 'No, of course not.'

'And do you have a bad temper?'

'Sometimes,' I said, 'when creeps like you annoy me.' And to my horror a blush spread from my

35

neck up to my forehead. How I hated myself for being so stupid.

'You've gone red,' he said, the serious look gone from his eyes. He bent to see my face, grinning like a Cheshire cat. He did a little dance.

'Red hair, red face – no wonder you're so fiery.'

'Shut up!' I gave him a filthy look and turned away. He might charm old ladies but he wouldn't charm me.

I began to run. Run and run. Wanting to get away from those eyes and that beastly smile. Wanting to escape the strange feeling that had crept over me like a roaring wind from nowhere.

I hardly ever wear shoes in hot weather and my bare feet flew across that grass as if they had wings. A herd of cows looked startled and scampered away, bucking, tails held high like banners announcing a carnival. I raced across the field and vaulted the gate. I wished I could run for ever and never have to see wretched Stephen again.

When I reached the bank of the creek I flung myself down on the grass. The tide was out and the water only a shining mirror of silver between high banks of mud. Further down, a line of motor cruisers lay at crazy angles.

Stephen arrived and threw himself down beside me. I knew he could have caught me easily if he had wanted to. He'd got cups for running and all sorts of other things.

'For a girl,' he said, panting, 'you can't half run.'

Now I'm one of those people who think girls

can do anything just as well as boys. That remark got my back up straight away.

'I'd break the record trying to get away from you,' I snapped.

'Really?'

'Yes, really.'

I turned on my stomach and buried my face in my arm.

'Are you crying?'

'Don't be stupid!' I looked up at him through my hair. He looked so worried that I had to laugh. Soon he was laughing too and we lay side by side laughing our insides out. It's funny but Stephen was always able to do that – turn my bad moods to good ones, my tears to laughter. I don't know how. No one ever could before. No one has since.

We stopped laughing and lay there melting in the sun. I shut my eyes and listened to a skylark singing way above our heads. The sound came and went, came and went. It reminded me of a dragon-fly flitting from plant to plant, lily to lily.

I sensed a movement and opened my eyes just enough to see Stephen sit up and take off his T-shirt. He had really broad shoulders, muscly arms. He lay down beside me, eyes closed, sighing a sigh of contentment. I wanted to stretch out my hand and touch him, stroke the blond hairs that glinted on his arm. The urge was like a pain deep in the pit of my stomach.

I shut my eyes again and breathed deeply. The feeling went away. My heart seemed to soar up and down with the skylark. I felt so warm and comfortable and peaceful that I wanted to lie there for ever.

I must have dozed off because the next thing I knew Stephen was leaning over me, saying something.

'Wake up, Red, we'll be late for dinner.'

'What did you call me?' I said without opening my eyes.

'Red . . . good, don't you think?'

To be honest I didn't think much of it but I'd been called a few things in my time and if that's what he wanted then who was I to argue?

I opened my eyes slowly. I thought stupid thoughts. I thought that if every day I could open them and see Stephen's face in front of me then I would never want anything else as long as I lived.

As he spoke he brushed some wisps of hair that stuck to my face. I thought for a minute he was going to kiss me. He had that look on his face that I'd seen on boys' faces before. I knew only too well what it meant. It frightened me. It excited me too but I wriggled away and jumped up.

'Come on then – let's go.'

Aunt Jo was gone. Only an empty cigarette packet, a few dog ends and a patch of flattened grass showed she'd been there. I picked up the packet and shoved it in the pocket of my jeans. I hate people who leave litter about.

'We'll try the boat tomorrow, shall we?' Stephen said.

'Okay – if it's fine.'

He looked at the sky.

'I think this weather will last all summer,' he said.

And he was right. It did.

Chapter Six

The next day I had a call from Julie. I suppose you might call Julie my best friend. She lived on the other side of the village and my father knew her parents. She was really the only one in my class I had much in common with and even that wasn't a great deal. We visited each other from time to time in the holidays. I'd forgotten all about her up till now.

She invited me to stay for a few days. I didn't really want to go but I thought a day or two away from Stephen might do me good. Help me get my feelings for him sorted out. I found I was thinking about him more and more and I didn't want to – it scared me. I had always thought there were lots of things I wanted to do with my life before I started thinking seriously about love and sex and all that stuff.

'What about the boat?' he asked when I told him I'd decided to go.

I shrugged. 'It'll still be here when I get back – go on your own if you want.'

He looked disappointed and I felt a bitch for hurting him. I almost changed my mind.

'Anyway, I'm only going for a day or two,'

I said, trying to make him feel better.

'Can't your friend come here instead?'

'No,' I said quickly, selfishly wanting Stephen all to myself.

'Okay then.' It was his turn to shrug. 'It doesn't matter.'

But I knew it did.

I told myself it was no good caring about him. He'd be going back to school in September and I wouldn't see him again until Christmas. He'd forget about me anyway. It was just no good.

'If I get my car in time I'll come and pick you up if you like,' Stephen said suddenly. 'When you want to come home I mean.'

'I didn't know you were getting a car,' I said, surprised he hadn't mentioned it before.

'Some insurance or something – comes out when I'm eighteen but Mum's letting me have the money early.'

'Can you drive then?'

'I learned at school.'

I thought then that this school of his must be really great if they taught you to drive.

'Okay,' I said. 'I'll give you a ring when I want to come back.'

As it turned out I was really bored at Julie's. It used to be good fun going there – we used to have a great time with her parents and brothers. This time though they had gone away and we were alone in the house. All she wanted to do was stay in and play records and stuff like that.

The second night she invited a couple of boys over for the evening. I was angry when I found out they were coming.

'For goodness' sake, Ju,' I said, 'you know I hate them – why didn't you ask me if I minded?'

'Because I knew what you'd say. Oh come on, Rina, you never *are* interested in boys, what's the matter with you – are you gay or something?'

'Don't be stupid – I just like to pick my own friends, that's all. Anyway, they're only interested in one thing – you know that.'

'These two aren't like that.'

'Who're you kidding? They're *all* like that!'

They brought a bottle of wine and a pile of records. I just sat in the corner and sulked. I suppose it was mean, spoiling Julie's evening but I wished she'd asked me first.

After a couple of hours trying to fob off exploring hands and wine-stinking breath I stormed off to bed leaving Julie to cope with them both. Half an hour later I heard the front door slam. Julie charged up the stairs and threw open the bedroom door.

'I thought you were my friend,' she said angrily, throwing herself down on the bed. 'Fancy leaving me with both of them.'

'I don't know how you can let them put their hands all over you, especially that one with greasy hair,' I said in disgust. 'It's not even as if you care about him.'

'For God's sake, Rina, it's just a bit of fun.'

'Well, it's not my idea of fun.'

'Well, what is, for God's sake? It strikes me you're getting to be as crazy as your aunt.'

That really hurt. 'If you mean I'm different – well then, I am – you should know that, Julie. If you were my real friend then you'd know it and would stop trying to make me into something I'm not.'

Half an hour later we were still arguing. In the end we both ended up apologising. We were always quarrelling anyway. It was nothing new.

Then I told her about Stephen.

'Ah-ha,' she said, grinning knowingly, 'so that's why you haven't phoned me, I wondered what was up with you. And that's why you wouldn't have anything to do with Andy – why didn't you say something before?'

'There was nothing to say.'

'Oh yes!'

I was beginning to get angry again. 'Anyway it's not that, Ju – I just need to *love* someone before I . . . you know.'

'Well, it sounds as if you love Stephen all right.' She giggled.

Right at that moment I hated her. How could I be in love with him anyway? He was just a good friend, that's all. Why spoil things? Why was I so angry when Julie suggested I loved him? Anyway, I was in love with Rod Stewart – that didn't cause any problems. I thought he was wonderful – he didn't know I existed. What possible complications could there be in that kind of relationship? Julie should know me better.

She sat on the edge of the bed and looked at herself in the mirror. Her face was flushed from the wine, her eyes bright.

'I nearly did it tonight,' she said casually, taking off her earrings and peering closely at her complexion.

'Did what?'

'What do you *think?*' she said scathingly. 'Really, Rina, sometimes I think you don't live in this world at all.'

'You mean you . . . '

'That's right, in the other room while you were trying to fob off Andy.'

'For God's sake, Julie.'

'He didn't have anything with him, you know . . . contraceptives, so I wouldn't let him.'

'But you don't love him, do you . . . ?'

She turned. 'Rina, you're so old-fashioned. We're both nearly seventeen and neither of us have done it yet. We're about the only two in our class who haven't. I *want* to know what it's like Rina. I *want* to know.'

I didn't tell her that *I* wanted to know, too.

'But you can't just do it with anyone, just to find out what it's like.'

'Why not?'

'Because you can't.'

'Well, I'm going to – soon. People will think I'm some kind of freak.'

'I don't care what people think.'

Julie looked at me in the mirror. 'No, you don't, do you?'

'No – people should mind their own business.'

I turned over and buried my face in the pillow. I wished Julie would shut up. I wished she'd go away. I wished I had stayed at home.

I felt better in the morning. Things always seem better when you've slept on them. It's as if sleep washes away your anger.

'Let's go for a bike ride,' I said after breakfast. I was bored with playing records. Bored with staying indoors.

'Do we have to?' Julie leaned back in her chair, stretching out her legs. 'I've got a headache.'

'Serves you right for drinking all that wine.'

'You had some too.'

'Not as much as you.'

'Some friend you are.' She went to the sink and filled a glass with water. She put two tablets in and waited until they had dissolved.

'Shall we then? Fresh air's better for a headache than those drugs you're stuffing yourself with.'

Actually I had a headache too, although I wasn't letting on. Dreams of Stephen had haunted my mind all night and although I didn't feel angry any more I wanted to get out in the air to blow the shadows away.

Julie sighed like a martyr. 'Okay, if you really want to.' She was used to me bullying her. I think she really quite enjoyed it. She had trouble making decisions on her own. 'You'll have to have my brother's bike though.'

We decided to go down to the creek. I suppose,

45

secretly, I hoped Stephen might be there with the boat.

Although the day was hot the sky was overcast, heavy as lead. There must have been a plague of those little black beetles because as we rode along they got in our hair, in our eyes. Even up our noses. We kept having to stop to dig them out or blow our noses and hope they came down.

It was when Julie was trying to get one of the wretched things out of my eye that a car pulled up behind us. I heard Julie draw in her breath. Blinded as I was I couldn't see a flipping thing.

I heard Stephen's voice.

'You all right, Red?'

In spite of my streaming eye I grinned and held out my hand to feel for him. It came in contact with his arm. His flesh was warm. I let my hand stay there a minute.

'Fine,' I sniffed. 'Except for this great monster in my eye.'

He took the tissue from Julie. 'Let's have a try.'

Very gently he held my eye open with his thumb and dabbed away at the bug until it came out. All of a sudden I could see his face close to mine. I could see myself reflected in his eyes.

'There,' he said, showing me. A minute black speck on the tissue. 'Hardly a giant.'

'It felt like one.' I grinned. 'Thanks.'

He looked at Julie. Now, Julie was really pretty – much smaller-boned than me. Short black hair and eyes that are darkest blue like saucers in her face. Her lashes are curly and almost reach her eyebrows.

Against me, with my lanky legs, great mass of hair and green eyes and freckled nose I guess she looked like a rose beside a weed.

'This is Julie,' I said, although he must have known who she was. 'Ju, this is Stephen.' She must have known who he was too.

'Hello.' He smiled and held out his hand.

Julie looked a bit startled, blushed, took his hand and shook it limply.

'Hi,' she managed to mumble.

Then, to my surprise, his eyes didn't linger on her breasts (which are much bigger than mine). He looked straight back at me and said, 'Are you going to the creek?'

I said we were. Then I noticed he'd got the boat on top of the car. His car.

'You got the car then?' I said unnecessarily, as it obviously wasn't my father's, or Jean's.

'Yes . . . what do you think?'

'Looks okay.' (Afterwards Julie said I should have admired it. Having two brothers, she knew how men felt about their cars.) Actually it was just a car to me – an engine and four wheels, like any other.

Stephen reached the creek before us and was unloading the boat when we arrived. I gave him a hand. Julie just stood around watching, looking all doe-eyed at Stephen.

We put the boat into the water.

'Better leave it a bit – make sure it doesn't leak,' Stephen said.

We sat on the bank watching the tide. I didn't

47

say much. I was thinking about last night. Thinking about those awful boys and the things Julie had said. I wondered what made her like that. So desperate to know what sex was like she'd almost try it with anyone. Maybe she thought she was being left on the shelf.

She and Stephen chatted like old friends. He seemed to have a knack of making conversation with anyone – even people he didn't know. Or maybe it was just Julie's big boobs he was interested in after all.

When we could see the boat was okay Stephen asked who wanted to go out first. It was only big enough for two at a time.

'You go,' I said before Julie could answer. 'I'll sit here and watch.'

Julie hated boats but she went all the same.

I sat on the grass. I'd only got shorts and a T-shirt on and those wretched bugs were driving me mad. I wished I hadn't come. Sleep hadn't cured me after all. Last night had put me in a bad temper for the rest of the week.

I lay back and listened to the sounds of the river. It was so hot and there was no one about so I took off my T-shirt. The bugs drove me madder so I put it on again.

I sat up and looked for Stephen and Julie but the boat had gone round the bend in the river, out of sight. Suddenly I remembered I hadn't warned Stephen about the strong currents. I had visions of them being swept out to sea. Without bothering to put on my shoes I ran along the bank but to my relief Stephen had turned the boat and they were on their way back, rowing hard against the tide.

Seeing my anxious face he called out.

'What's wrong?'

'Nothing,' I shouted. He waved his arm and the boat rocked precariously. I saw Julie clutch the sides in alarm. I grinned to myself. She wasn't a hardened sailor like me.

I walked on a little way, enjoying the feeling of the warm turf beneath my toes. A breeze had sprung up. Blue sky was beginning to show through the clouds. The oppressiveness of the day had lifted, taking all the bugs back into the high atmosphere. Swallows screamed between the banks, wheeling and diving like space fighters. My headache had gone too.

I knew then, suddenly, that I would have to go home. I knew that Stephen and I had the whole glorious summer in front of us. Together. There were so many things I wanted to do. Row across to the bird sanctuary, show him the ruined church across the meadow, swim in the creek when the tide was high. All these hours I was spending with Julie playing records, watching boring old TV, talking about sex and stuff were nothing but a sheer waste of time. It was no good running away from Stephen. No good running away from the way I felt about him. He was here and I wanted more than anything else to be with him. That was that.

When I got back they were waiting. Julie didn't look very happy. She had got her jeans wet. Stephen had my shoes in his hand.

'I'm coming home tonight,' I said. 'Will you come and get me?'

'Sure – if that's what you want.'

Over Julie's head Stephen looked at me and smiled.

And that was the beginning of my *real* Stephen summer.

Chapter Seven

The first thing we did was open up the old summer-house. Out came the dusty old deckchairs. Out came the spiders and generations of dead flies. Out came the old sofa to be brushed and shampooed. It turned out to be quite a nice bit of furniture under all that gunge.

'It will give an air of elegance to the place,' Stephen said.

We looked at each other and laughed. Our faces were dirty, hair full of dust. We looked like two tramps who couldn't care a monkey's for elegance.

We turned the place into our studio. We took all our drawing things, easels, sketchbooks, paints. Aunt Jo gave us some of her sketches to put on the walls. Later we added some of our own. Blun fished out some old curtains and cushions for the sofa. We were like two children playing house.

I think those days were some of the happiest ever in my life. There were happier days to come, although I didn't know it at the time.

Being with Stephen had changed me somehow. I didn't feel so angry at everything. I didn't argue with my father, didn't even think nasty thoughts about the Grey person. In fact I quite got to like

51

her. It was only her obsessive love for Stephen that annoyed me. I suppose I was jealous.

We talked about everything, Stephen and me. About life, about our hopes, our dreams, love, even about sex. Somehow it didn't seem a waste of time talking about those things with him.

One day, when John and Jean and Aunt Jo had gone out for the day he asked me if I was a virgin.

'Yes,' I said and I knew I went a bit red.

'Lots of girls your age aren't.'

'I know that.'

'What are you waiting for?'

'No one's ever asked me,' I said, looking at him sideways.

He grinned. 'I bet.'

'It's true,' I insisted, 'no one I fancy anyway.'

'Don't you fancy anyone at school?'

'You *must* be joking – anyway, what about you?'

'I don't fancy anyone at school – I'm not gay.'

I punched him, laughing. 'I know that, stupid. I mean are you a virgin?'

He flushed. 'What do you want to know for?'

'Because you asked if I was,' I said indignantly.

'That's different.'

'It bloody well is not,' I yelled.

'Sssh,' he held his hand over my mouth. We were sitting down by the stream and there was no one anywhere to hear. I grabbed his arm and pulled his hand away. I squeezed as hard as I could. 'Come on – tell me!'

'Well, if you really want to know – I'm not.'

'Oh!'

52

I let go. I felt suddenly like a balloon that had been popped. I didn't know what to say. A kind of icy feeling came over me as if someone was slicing the top of my head off. I suppose it was shock. Stupid really. Someone like Stephen. He'd be bound to have had sex. But somehow I couldn't bear to think about it.

He must have seen the expression on my face. He must have read my thoughts.

'I didn't love her or anything. She was just a girl from the village near our school.'

That made me angry. At least I think it was anger I was feeling.

'What do you mean *just* a girl from the village – she had feelings too, didn't she?'

I must have been shouting although I didn't realise it at the time.

'Hey – calm down. I meant it wasn't anything serious. I just took her out a couple of times, that's all.'

'And you did it – after only seeing her twice?'

'She wanted me to.'

'Stephen, you could have got AIDS.'

'You're joking – I used a condom, I'm not that stupid.'

I knew my face was hot. I stood up, trembling. I hated the thought of him doing it. Fucking. I hated it, I hated him.

'I'm going in.'

He started after me. 'Red, Red, what's wrong?'

'Nothing.' I wrenched away from him. I was crying. I couldn't bear him to see.

I ran away. Through the garden, up the back stairs to my room. If he followed me I'd kill him.

I lay on my bed and wept. I knew it was stupid. I couldn't help it.

Eventually I stopped. I felt better. I realised just how crazily I was behaving. I washed my face and ran my fingers through my hair. In the mirror I looked awful.

I knew Stephen was in his room. I'd heard him run up and open his door very quietly and shut it again.

I tapped on his door. 'Stephen . . . ?'

'What?'

'Can I come in?'

He opened the door. He had taken off his T-shirt and stood there in just his jeans. His feet were bare. His hair had grown long over the holidays and the sun had bleached it in streaks the colour of vanilla ice-cream. His face was hard, angry. It was as if he knew I was the spoilt child he had first thought me to be.

I clenched my hands together and held them to my mouth.

'I'm sorry,' I said.

His face changed. His eyes softened. He put out a hand and touched my arm, then took it away quickly as if my skin had burned his finger-tips.

'I'm sorry too. I didn't mean it to sound like that. She was a nice girl – I liked her a lot.'

He thought I had been angry because I felt he had used her for his own pleasure. I was. But

54

there were other reasons too. Reasons I was only just beginning to understand.

He pulled me inside the room. 'Here.' He handed me a Coke.

We sat a while and listened to his tapes. We didn't say much. I don't know why but I couldn't look him in the face. He sat on the floor thumbing through a car magazine. There were posters of cars on the wall. An old Model-T. A Trans-am. The picture of Marilyn Monroe that had caused his downfall.

The phone rang and he went out on the landing to answer it.

'That was Jean,' he said when he came back. 'They're not coming home till late. We've got to get our own dinner.'

'Great.' I jumped off the bed, glad something had happened to break the ice. 'What do you fancy?'

He shrugged. 'Don't know – let's see what there is.'

Stephen prepared a salad while I cooked a couple of steaks we'd found in the fridge. Blun had left some buns fresh out of the oven on the worktop. I munched a couple while I watched the grill. I thought about the days when my father used to work late and Aunt Jo cooked for us.

'I hate cooking,' I said.

'Do you? I don't mind it actually. I used to have to cook for myself during the holidays. Mind you, I hated eating alone – I couldn't wait to get back to school.'

'Did your mother visit you much?'

'Most weekends – Sundays anyway. Your father came several times, did you know?'

'No.' I frowned. 'You know, it's funny, he never said a word to me about Jean, or you. I wonder why.'

'He was probably scared.'

'What of?' I took the grill pan out and turned the meat. It spat at me like an angry cat.

'Well – of what you'd think.'

'I did hate it when he first told me,' I admitted. 'But I can see how happy it's made him. Having you here, having Jean. You're almost like a son to him.'

'Do you mind?'

'A bit – but I'll get used to it.'

'*We* wouldn't have met if they hadn't got together.'

'No.'

He put the salad bowl on the table and came to watch the steaks with me.

'So you don't mind being my little sister after all?'

I tried to stab him with the fork but he ducked out of the way. 'Not so much of the little!' I said, thinking the last thing in the world I wanted to be was his sister.

The steaks were done. I shoved them on to our plates. 'I hope these are okay.'

'I'm sure they'll be wonderful,' he said sarcastically, dodging away before I could kick him.

We ate in silence. When he had finished Stephen

56

leaned back in his chair and put his hands behind his head.

'It's great, isn't it? – being here on our own. Just the two of us.'

'Yes.' I scraped the fat from my steak into the bin. At the bottom were the remains of one of Jo's bird cakes. If they didn't stick together she refused to put them on the birdtable. Blun or I usually rescued them and threw them over the hedge where Jo couldn't see.

'You know what I'd like to do,' Stephen said.

'No – what?'

'Go off camping somewhere – to Wales, somewhere like that.'

'On your own?'

'No, with you, stupid.'

I looked at him. Excitement surged through me. What a fantastic idea. Just the two of us. But they wouldn't let us – I knew it. Or would they?

'Do you think they'd let us?'

'It might cause a bit of a stink but we could ask.'

I didn't care if it caused a stink. Suddenly it was the thing I most wanted to do in all the world. We hadn't had a proper holiday for years. My father was always too busy – a workaholic Jean called him, although he spent much more time at home now she was there.

We began to make plans. Stephen went to his room and brought down some maps. We spread them out on the kitchen table and planned our route. I was so excited I felt like a child again.

The next thing we did was to go up into the

attic and dig out a couple of tents. My father used to let me camp in the garden when I was small. I loved lying out there listening to the sounds of the night. Blun thought he was mad, letting me. I was never frightened, not once.

The tents smelt musty so we spread them out on the lawn to air.

When my father and Jean and Aunt Jo came back we told them what we wanted to do. My father didn't like the idea. I knew he wouldn't.

Stephen reassured him. 'I've been on outward bound lots of times with the school,' he said. 'I'll look after Rina, I promise.'

'I can look after myself,' I said indignantly.

'That's just the sort of attitude I worry about,' my father said, frowning. Stephen started to say something but I threw him a warning glance. I knew exactly how to handle my father. I was too much like him not to know – that's why we argued so much.

'Oh Daddy,' I said, 'we'll be fine, honestly. You used to let me camp out when I was small. Nothing can possibly go wrong.'

'That was slightly different,' my father growled, 'you were always within calling distance.'

Jean put her hand on his arm. 'They'll be all right, John,' she said. 'Stephen has lots of experience – he takes the younger boys climbing every year, don't you darling?'

'That's right – we even go in winter when the weather's unpredictable.'

Jean smiled at her son. My father looked at her

and I noticed how soft his eyes were. I felt a stab of jealousy. I looked away quickly. It was stupid to feel like that. Knowing it was stupid didn't make it any easier though.

'How long will you be away?' my father asked and I knew by the tone of his voice that he was going to give in.

'A week at most,' Stephen said.

My father looked at me, then at Stephen.

'You'll look after her . . . ?'

'God, Daddy . . . !'

This time Stephen threw me a warning glance.

'Of course I will.'

'All right then. But you must tell us exactly where you're going and promise to ring us whenever you can.'

I was so delighted I threw my arms around my father and hugged him. Surprisingly he hugged me back and we all laughed. It was almost as if we were one, big, happy family.

Before we went Blun came to my room and gave me a lecture. Or tried to at least. I was packing my stuff into a rucksack. Spare pair of jeans, shorts, a couple of T-shirts, several pairs of pants and a toothbrush.

'Don't forget to take a thick jumper,' she said.

'It won't be cold, Blun – this weather's going to last for ever.'

'It *can* turn very nasty on those Welsh moors. Now do as I say, and take your kagoule too.'

I sighed but put them in to humour her.

'Rina . . . ' she hesitated. I looked up from trying to stuff the last things into the bag. 'Rina . . . I feel I must give you a little talk before you go. Now really it's your father's place but he's always left these things to me, as you know.'

Oh no, I thought, not the birds and bees, please Blun.

'You're not going to lecture me, please darling Blun.' I looked at her and grinned. 'You know I *am* almost seventeen – I do know the facts of life.' In fact I probably know more about them than you, I added to myself.

'I know that, dear,' she looked embarrassed. Poor Blun. I sat on the bed next to her and put my arm through hers.

'Dear Blun, please don't give me a little talk – I *know* what you're going to say and you needn't worry. I'm quite old enough to look after myself.'

'I'm not saying you're not – it's just that I don't want to see you get yourself into any kind of situation you can't cope with.'

'I won't – I'll be a good girl, I promise.'

'I know you might intend to but Stephen is a very handsome young man and . . . '

I put my finger against her lips. ' . . . and he's a very upright, moral, privately educated person.'

'You're laughing at me.'

'Really, Blun,' I was laughing, I couldn't help it. 'Don't worry about me, okay?' I kissed her.

'All right then, I'll try not to.' In spite of herself she smiled.

She helped me finish packing and carried my

sleeping bag down to the hall. Stephen's stuff was already there. I wondered if anyone had tried to give him a little talk. I made a mental note to ask him.

We loaded up the mini with our gear. There seemed much too much to carry but Stephen said we'd manage okay. He had his head under the bonnet, checking the oil.

'I'll just go up and say goodbye to Aunt Jo,' I said.

'Okay.'

Aunt Jo wasn't well. Some kind of summer 'flu I think. Things like that always went to her chest and gave her chronic bronchitis. This was no exception.

I knocked on her door and a funny, squeaky voice told me to come in.

Jo's room was really weird. Like the inside of a witch's cave. She kept the curtains drawn most of the time, which was strange. She loved light and air. It was almost as if she was afraid that too much of it might invade her privacy.

Although she had lived with me all my life I had only been in her room perhaps half a dozen times that I could remember.

In one corner was a large chest of drawers. Half of them were open and stuff hung out like creatures emerging from inside. Coloured scarves, knitted tights, all sorts of things. On the top was an array of photographs in old-fashioned frames. There was a vase of wild flowers, like an altar or some kind of shrine. The photographs were of her dead lover. I felt my eyes being strangely drawn towards them. I was curious about him – always had been ever since I could remember but had never liked to ask her about him. I knew he had been killed in the war. What had made him so fantastic that she never found anyone to replace him? Why had she never married but had devoted her life to my father? I really would ask her one day.

There were other pictures there too. Ones she had painted. Bright colours, flowers, landscapes, some ponies in the field. On the mantelpiece over the fireplace was a photograph of a young Stephen in cricket clothes. I guessed Jean must have given it to her. I knew Aunt Jo was fond of him. Always charming her with his wide, wicked, winning smile. His hair was fairer than ever when he was young.

I was just going over to get a closer look when she called me from the bed. 'Katharine.' (Katharine's my real name, after my mother, but Jo was the only person who ever called me that.) 'Have you come to say goodbye?'

'Yes, Aunt Jo, we're just off.' I went and sat at the foot of the bed. The room smelt musty and dry. The dryness seemed to invade my skin and I shuddered involuntarily. I wrinkled my nose. Jo smelt musty too – like a pile of old leaves left over from autumn.

'How are you feeling?' I asked. She looked awful. She shifted her position against the pillows. The book she had been reading fell to the floor. I picked it up. It was a volume of poetry of the First

World War. I had read some myself. Some of it was beautiful and sad and full of pity. I still have that book. It still makes me cry – even on days when I think there are no tears left.

'A bit better today, I think.' She sniffed, not sounding any better at all.

'You'll be up and about by the time we get back,' I said, feeling sorry for her having to be shut up in this mausoleum when the world was so beautiful outside.

'I hope so.' She sighed and the noise was like wheezy old bellows pumping up a fire. 'Get my purse from the dressing table, will you dear?' I rose and fetched it for her. On the way back I looked at the photographs of her lover.

'Will you tell me about him one day, Aunt Jo?' I asked, lingering over one of him in army uniform. He was very good-looking.

'When you have time to listen. You young people are always so busy.' She flapped her hand in the air impatiently like a bony bird trying to escape. I decided to make her tell me when we got back from our camping trip. Talking about him might help exorcise the ghost. I wondered if, in all the years since he died, she had ever talked about him. I don't suppose my father would have wanted to listen. He had only been a baby and there was no one else. Unless she had spoken about him to my mother – I'd probably never know. It's wicked not to talk about people when they've died. It makes it seem as if they never existed. After all, if I had never talked about my mother it would seem as if her life on earth had been of no importance. As if no one at all remembered her.

Aunt Jo fished about inside her purse and took out a fiver. 'Here,' she said, shoving it into my hand. 'Buy yourself something nice on your holiday.'

I didn't want the money but couldn't hurt her feelings.

'That's great,' I said, 'thanks, Aunt Jo.' On impulse I leaned forward and kissed her musty cheek. Her skin felt slightly moist and warm. I was surprised. I had imagined it would feel rough and dry. I couldn't remember how long it was since I had last kissed her. It must have been years.

I tried to stand up but she held my arm. Her eyes looked watery as if she was about to cry. It seemed as if she was trying to say something but couldn't. I waited.

'I must go, Aunt Jo,' I said eventually. 'Stephen's waiting.'

'Rina . . . there's something I must . . . ' she broke off. 'Never mind, it'll keep. Have a lovely time – be happy.'

It seemed a strange thing for her to say but I thought then that perhaps Aunt Jo, of all people, understood about my feelings for Stephen. I realised she must have been only about my age when she met her lover. No wonder she had mourned so when he died. The thought made me shiver – as if someone had walked over my grave. I couldn't get out of the room quickly enough. As I turned to close the door gently I caught another glimpse of the photograph of Stephen. His eyes followed me, familiar eyes, eyes it seemed that I had known all my life.

They all stood at the gate waving as we drove off down the road. Blun, Mr Blun, Jean, my father. Jean and my father stood very close, lovers, his arm protectively round her shoulder. I wonder what she really thought about her beloved son going off with me. I wondered if she honestly believed he would look after me and protect me as if I was his little sister.

When we were out of sight I leaned back in the seat and stretched out my arms.

'Free,' I said, 'free at last!'

Stephen grinned. 'Three cheers.'

'Did you get a lecture?'

'What about?'

'The birds and the bees.'

'God no. Did you?'

'Nearly – I nipped it in the bud.'

He laughed. 'I got a bit of a talk about being sensible, that's all.'

'Oh God, Stephen, have you ever been anything *but* sensible?'

'You'd be surprised.'

'Well, with you being such a sensible person and me being only a child we should get on very well.'

He laughed again.

I often wonder now, lying lonely on my bed and all the world as black as night, if my father and Jean really did imagine we were children. I wonder if it never once occurred to them what really might happen to Stephen and me on that holiday. I wonder if all they were afraid of was that we might catch cold, or fall, or not wash, or not have enough to eat. All those trivial things that parents worry about when their children leave, when they go off to the wilderness to fend for themselves.

I wonder if they really thought that only they, as adults, felt things, or had emotions, or had hearts that might easily be broken?

Chapter Eight

Stephen knew a place near Llanerfyl that was good for hiking, so that's where we went. We parked the car and unloaded our gear.

'We'd better take the waterproofs,' Stephen said. 'It can't half rain here.'

'It won't rain,' I said, so sure. 'We're going to have the most gorgeous week, I know it.'

'Sometimes I think you're some kind of witch,' he grumbled, putting the things back in the boot. 'If we get pneumonia it'll be your fault.'

I waved my hands around, making a spell.

'I am a witch so you'd better watch out – I'll turn you into a frog – I'm fed up with you being a prince.'

He grinned. 'I'll show you what kind of prince I am.'

'Promises, promises.'

Our eyes met and in the end I had to look away. I don't know what it was that passed between us – a kind of suppressed excitement, a kind of chemical reaction. What I saw in Stephen's eyes scared me a bit, made my heart beat fast, filled me with anticipation.

'I'll help you on with your pack,' he said.

I turned round so he could heave it up on my back. He lifted my hair so it wouldn't get caught in the straps. I felt him rub it between his fingers softly before he let go. I gave the pack a final hitch up.

'Okay?'

'Um – fine.' I staggered a bit.

Stephen laughed. 'Witches are supposed to have superhuman strength.'

'It's fine – really.'

I didn't want him to know it was almost killing me.

He locked the car and we set off.

The road, narrow, grey like a ribbon winding its way up into the hills, got steeper and steeper as it went. Gradually I slowed, stopping once or twice to wipe the sweat from my face. Stephen, miles ahead, apparently oblivious to the heat, turned and called, 'You okay?'

'Great.' Sweating, I struggled to catch him up.

He waited and took my hand when I finally caught up with him. 'Do you want to rest?'

'No.' I was annoyed at my own weakness. 'Let's get to the top.'

Stephen studied the map. 'Once we get to the top of this lane the ground flattens out. We can walk for miles across the moor – look,' he pointed, 'there's a lake here where we can camp the night.'

'Looks great.'

Stephen tucked the map into the back pocket of his shorts and took my hand again. We walked on, slower now, shoulders touching.

'Have you been here before?' I asked.

'Not here – places like it though. I love Wales. I suppose it's all the open space after being cooped up at school all term.' He took a deep breath and blew the air out noisily through his nostrils. 'I'm really the sort of person who needs open spaces.'

'Me too – Canada, those great prairies – I'd love to go there.'

'And Australia.'

'Oh yes – how about a sheep farm with millions of acres – so much land you could ride all day and not see another soul.'

'Sounds wonderful.'

'I can't imagine your mother being very pleased if you became a sheep farmer.'

Stephen made a face. 'Nor me – she has such great ambitions for me it feels like a great weight on my head.'

'Poor Stephen.'

He shrugged. 'I suppose it's because I'm all she's had. I know she's always done her best for me but sometimes I feel suffocated, sometimes I just want to get away.'

'You do get away – all the time.'

'You know what I mean.'

I sighed. 'Yes – but it's not so bad now, is it? Now you've got a proper home and family?'

He squeezed my hand. 'No – in fact I don't even want to go back – the first time I can remember feeling like that.'

I didn't say anything. I didn't want to think

about Stephen going back to school. I put it away into a corner of my mind and shut the door.

We walked along in silence after that. I stole a glance at Stephen's face – it was cool and serene. It was as if he belonged to these hills. He sensed me looking at him.

'Are you okay?'

'Fine.'

He squeezed my hand again.

A small group of pony-trekkers passed us on their way down from the moor. The ponies were fat and tired. Perched on their backs were scared-looking holiday-makers with kagoules tied round their waists and riding hats too big. They smiled and said 'Hello' and 'What a lovely day it is.' We turned and watched them wend their way down the road. The ponies slipped now and then and bright sparks flew from their hooves. When they had gone, turning out of sight round the bend, it seemed as if we were the last people on earth.

Soon the road petered out into a stony track and stretching before us was an endless landscape of bracken-clad, undulating moorland. I had got slower and slower and redder and redder in the face. Stephen laughed at me and said I was unfit. I noticed he slowed his pace to keep level with me, though.

At last we topped the hill. The climb had been worth every minute. It was as if all the world was spreadeagled below us. Miles on miles of patterned moorland purple and green with summer. In the distance more hills, some shadowed with dark green pines that cut the horizon in two. In the far distance the sea was a spark of silver between two hills and the sun shot shafts towards the ground like escape routes from heaven.

'Let's rest now,' Stephen said.

I slipped off my pack and plonked down on the grass with a sigh. Here we were truly alone. Nothing, no one but each other and the sheep and foxgloves and a ruined shepherd's hut stark against the sky. The breeze touched my face like the kiss of life. I turned to Stephen lying stretched out, eyes closed.

'Stephen, it's so wonderful up here, it takes my breath away.'

He looked at me lazily through half-opened eyes. 'I thought you'd like it, even though the climb nearly killed you.'

I kicked his leg. 'Pig.'

I got up and walked away from him. I stretched my arms wide, feeling the wind through my fingertips. I whirled like a windmill to all four corners of the world. I tried to speak, wanting to tell Stephen how I felt, but the words wouldn't come.

Stephen sat up and watched me. The wind blew my hair out behind me. I raised my hands and held it away from my face. When I looked at Stephen he had a strange expression on his face. He held out his hand and I went to him.

'What's wrong?'

'Nothing,' he said, looking away.

We were so close I could smell the faint odour of his perspiration. There were beads of moisture on

71

his upper lip. His profile was serious as he looked across the moors.

Then he looked back at me and I almost drowned in his eyes. My heart gave a great antelope leap and began to beat loud, like a drum, echoing across the hills and valleys to the sea. I knew by the look in his eyes what he was going to do and nothing and nobody on earth could have dragged me away from that moment.

He put a hand either side of my face. I don't know why – it was probably the wind – but a tear crept from the corner of my eye and ran down my cheek. He wiped it away with his thumb. Then, pushing aside a strand of hair that had blown across my mouth, he leaned forward and kissed me. Gently, his lips just touching, soft, like a feather. I knew about kissing but not that it could ever be like that.

He drew back. I could see that he was breathing deeply. I smiled. It was so right for him to kiss me. The perfect thing to do in this perfect place. I put my hand up and touched his hair. My fingers trembled. He kissed me again. Longer now. Not so gentle and it seemed as if all the oceans of the world tumbled over my heart. Eventually he drew away.

'I've wanted to do that for a long time,' he murmured, his voice sounding all croaky and funny.

'Have you?' My voice was funny too.

'Didn't you know?'

I looked down, suddenly shy. 'I knew I wanted you to but I didn't know if you wanted to or not.'

72

He moved towards me again. I put my hands against his chest.

'We'll never reach the lake before dark if we don't get a move on,' I said. I knew that however perfect it seemed, up here with Stephen, it wasn't the right time or the right place but that the right time and the right place would soon come and when they did I'd be ready. I touched his cheek. 'We've got a whole week,' I added.

He grinned suddenly, the serious look fading from his eyes. He made a mock salute. 'Whatever you say, sir!'

He got up and pulled me up with him. I staggered – for some stupid reason my knees had turned to jelly. He steadied me with his hand.

'Drunk again?'

'No such luck,' I said.

When we had our packs on he put his hand casually on my shoulder.

'Okay?'

'Fine.'

We walked on. His hand stayed on my shoulder as if that was the place it had always wanted to be. As we walked I felt a closeness, a closeness that I had never felt before in all my life, a closeness you usually only feel in dreams. Only this was no dream. Me and Stephen together, knowing it was right, knowing it was for ever.

Or so, in my innocence, I thought at the time.

Chapter Nine

It was beginning to get dark when we reached the lake. There was a sign that said 'No fishing' but nothing about camping so that's where we decided to put up the tents.

The lake was fed by a stream that came singing and tumbling over rocks down the slope, the water pure and cold as ice.

We had walked in silence. I still felt strange from that kiss. Once or twice I caught Stephen looking at me and we smiled at each other, no words needed.

I lit the camp cooker while Stephen put the tents up. I filled the saucepan with water from the stream and started to make coffee. In the distance a curlew called and high above a buzzard dipped and wheeled on currents of air. The wind had dropped and there was a feeling of peace and utter loneliness in the air. I sat, hugging my knees, looking up at the sky. It had that curious deep-red glow of fine summer evenings as if there was a huge city somewhere beyond the horizon and the sky was illuminated by its lights.

Stephen came and squatted beside me. He took a mug of coffee and held it between his hands.

'Are the tents okay?'

'Fine.'

We drank our coffee in silence. For the first time since I'd known him I couldn't think of anything to say. I shivered. He turned his head to look at me.

'Not cold are you?'

'No – a ghost walked over my grave, that's all.'

He touched my arm. 'Do you mind if I walk a bit before we eat?'

'No – why should I?'

'No reason.'

I did mind really. I couldn't understand why he wanted to go off on his own. We'd been walking for hours, I thought he'd be glad to have a rest.

I watched him go. Head down, hands thrust deep in his pockets. It was as if he had some great problem he couldn't solve. A bird flew up from the heather, its alarm cry cutting deep into the twilight air. A group of startled sheep scampered away, their silly worried voices echoing down the hillside.

I watched Stephen until he disappeared, then rummaged about in the rucksack for the tin-opener.

While the beans were heating I decided to go for a swim. I stood up but couldn't see Stephen anywhere. The water looked so inviting – just the smell of it made me want to dive in. I felt sticky and smelly from our long, hot climb.

We hadn't thought to bring swimming stuff so I just kept my pants on. I hardly ever wear a bra. I don't need any elastic contraption to stop my breasts from drooping. Besides a bra makes me feel as if I'm wearing a straitjacket and I love to be free.

I turned the gas low under the saucepan and went to the water's edge. I put my toe in warily, holding my breath. It was cold, freezing, but I was determined to go in anyway.

I ran in and dived under. For a moment my breath disappeared completely but then, suddenly, it was wonderful. I turned on my back and floated, looking up at the darkening sky. The water felt marvellous against my skin – sensual, as if it had soft fingers caressing me. I looked down and could just see my breasts sticking up out of the water, nipples erect. It must have been the cold. I had just begun to daydream when I heard a shout from the bank.

'Rina – for Christ's sake!'

I rolled over and swam towards him.

'What?'

'You don't know how deep it is out there – what happens if you get cramp? Come out!'

'Not likely.'

I turned and swam away. I had never heard Stephen so angry before. Let him stew, I thought. I'm quite capable of looking after myself.

Next minute I heard a splash and he was swimming strongly towards me. He grabbed me and we both went under. We came up spluttering. Stephen tossed the water from his eyes. He looked different, older, his hair darkened, plastered against his head.

'Red, you bloody scared me.'

76

'It's okay, Stephen, don't be silly.'

His grip tightened. 'I'm not being silly. I'm supposed to be looking after you.'

'You do take your duties seriously – are you a prefect?'

I slipped away from him and swam towards the centre of the lake. To hell with him, I thought, he's as bad as my father, treating me like a child.

But – of course – he was good at swimming like everything else. When he caught me I pushed him under. He dragged me down with him, then up again. We both spluttered and gasped.

'Why are you so angry?' I shouted.

He looked at me for a minute then his expression changed. He turned back into the old Stephen again. Just like that, as if an elf had waved her magic wand. Maybe there were fairies here, or elves, or Hobbits – it seemed a magic place.

'I'm sorry.' He shook the water from his face.

'That doesn't answer my question.'

'You frightened me, that's all. I didn't know where you were.'

'Did you think I would leave you?' I put my arms around his neck and he pulled me close. Kissing me. We went under again and came up breathing, breathless.

'Come on,' he said at last, 'let's get out, it's cold.'

He reached the edge first and clambered out. He waited, his body silhouetted against the sky. He reached out his hand for me and as we stood together I could feel the whole outline of his body against mine. I'd already realised he was entirely naked but now it was different. Now there was no need to tread water to keep afloat. Nothing to stop us being so close that we seemed to melt together, one body, one person, fused by white, moonbright heat.

Stephen buried his face in my shoulder. I smelt the mountain water in his hair and a great wave of excitement and anticipation broke over me. I trembled.

'You're cold.'

'No . . .'

He put his hand on my breast. It felt warm. His fingers trembled slightly.

'We should eat,' he murmured, his mouth against mine.

'Yes,' thinking food was the last thing I wanted.

He drew away. He picked up my towel and threw it to me.

'The beans are burning anyway,' he said, grinning, breaking the magic spell of sexuality he had woven around me.

They were just about edible.

Sitting there, Stephen with a towel round his hips, me with wet hair and wet pants, I began to giggle.

'What are you laughing at?'

'I was just thinking what Daddy and Jean would say if they could see us now.'

'They wouldn't trust me again, that's for sure.'

I put down my plate and went to sit close. I put my arm through his. 'Oh come on, Stephen, it's not your fault.'

78

'Yes, it is, I shouldn't have kissed you like that.'
He threw his plate down on the ground and stood up, his back towards me.

'I'm not a child,' I said. I always seemed to be saying that lately, trying to convince everyone. I don't know why I bothered.

'I know but you're still only sixteen.'

I got up and took his hand. I laid it against my breast. Water fell from my hair. He turned with a strange, tragic expression on his face.

'I wish we hadn't come – I knew what would happen – I knew I wouldn't be able to help . . . ' His voice was low, muffled.

'You don't mean that.'

' . . . No.'

I touched his shoulder and there were goose bumps on his skin. 'We'd better dry off or we'll get pneumonia.'

I took the towel from my shoulders and rubbed my hair. Stephen went to wash the plates in the stream. I got the sleeping bags from the tents and zipped them together.

He came back. 'What are you doing?'

'Let's sleep out here, under the stars. It's so beautiful.'

'Red, I . . . ' I could see the fight he was having with himself.

'Don't you want to?'

'Red, I promised . . . '

'If you promised to look after me then you wouldn't want me to sleep alone would you?'

He groaned and pulled me towards him, his

arms going round me so tightly I could hardly breathe.

'Hey,' I struggled. 'Don't crush me to death.'

He lessened his hold. 'You are a witch, I know you are.'

I laid my head beneath his chin. It fitted there perfectly. He felt so warm, so safe. I wanted to stay there for ever.

His hands moved over my back and through my hair. It seemed I was an instrument, a violin, and he, the musician, was playing a symphony with the strings of my heart.

Later, in the moonlight, he turned his face towards me and I could see fear in his eyes. A cold wind swept out of nowhere and I shivered. He drew me closer. I was afraid and I didn't know why.

'What's wrong, Stephen?' I whispered, though there were only a few rabbits and one or two dozy sheep to hear.

He laid his mouth against my hair. 'I don't know – I'm just scared.'

'What of?'

'Your father – if he finds out.'

'Are you sorry then, are you sorry we've made love?'

'No – of course not!' He kissed me. 'How can I be sorry, I love you, I always have.'

'Even when I was shitty?'

He smiled. 'Even then.'

'I hated you because you were so gorgeous.'

He laughed then and tickled me. I fought him,

kicking his legs until he stopped. We clung together beneath the stars like children. Over his shoulder I saw the lake.

'Look!' I sat up.

'What?'

On the surface of the water the moon was reflected. A perfect, shining orb, shimmering, catchable. I slid out of the sleeping bag and went down to the water's edge. The night was balmy and the air seemed to kiss my skin. I felt bumps rise along my arms and across the back of my neck. There *was* magic here, I knew it.

Stephen appeared beside me like a pale god in the moonlight.

'When I was small,' I said, leaning against him, 'I used to think I could catch the moon in my hands.' I crouched and rippled the surface of the lake. Just for a moment the moon broke into a thousand pieces. It was as if someone had shattered a dream.

When the water stilled it was there again. It seemed symbolic – the end of my childhood, the beginning of something new, something so momentous, so exciting it made me tremble to think about it.

'Don't be afraid, Stephen,' I said, turning in his arms. 'Everything will be all right, I know it will. We love each other – what else matters?'

He kissed me. 'Nothing,' he said, 'nothing else matters.'

I shall always remember that night. I can't see a

reflection of the moon without thinking about it. I don't have any illusions now, though. I know you can't catch a mirage in your hands and I know there are lots of other things that matter in the world, besides love.

Chapter Ten

Stephen had used the only contraceptive he'd had with him so we went to a village chemist to get some more. I thought he would be embarrassed asking for condoms but he went in without batting an eyelid. I waited outside. Mind you, he did come out with a packet of Elastoplast as well.

I giggled. 'They won't be much good for preventing babies.'

'No – but they'll stop the blood if you get too passionate and scratch me to death.'

I went a bit red when he said that.

He grinned and put his arms round me, his mouth searching for mine. We must have looked daft, standing there, kissing, with great packs on our backs. Like two tortoises necking.

While we were in the village we found a phone box and called home. I knew it was one of Blun's days to come to the house. She told us Aunt Jo was still poorly and that my exam results had come. She opened the envelope while we waited. I'd passed them all – even maths. You could have knocked me down with a feather.

'Brilliant!' Stephen said, hugging me.

I hugged him back. '*You're* brilliant,' I said.

* * *

We must have walked a million miles that week. Stephen had planned the route in a big circle so the last night we ended up by the lake again.

I think it was the happiest time ever of my life. For a long time those memories were the only thing that kept me from drowning.

We sat by the water the last evening, reliving our week together.

I liked best the day we hadn't walked at all. It had been too hot – practically the hottest day we'd had all summer. We found a stream with deep, black pools where brown trout basked like miniature whales. Stephen had tried to tickle one but all he ended up doing was falling in the water. We had swum in those pools, stretching out to dry side by side on the big flat rocks that overhung the pool. Stephen said I reminded him of a water nymph he had seen once in a painting, naked in the pool, hair streaming out behind me like fronds of dark-red water weed.

When I think of it now the memory is like a song.

Stephen said he liked the day we'd stopped to photograph some wild ponies and lain afterwards in the murmurous, purple heather. I had sketched him lying asleep, arm flung up behind his head like a baby. He looked so young, his hair bleached blonder than ever. I remember I had this feeling I must go and lie beside him and take him in my arms. He'd woken, surprised, then he had smiled and held me close. So warm. So safe. The drawing was the best I'd ever done.

Better even than the one of my father I'd put on my bedroom wall.

We spent that last night out under the stars again. It was a sacred place for us. I wanted to put up a notice – 'Here Stephen and Rina made love for the very first time' – but he wouldn't let me.

I remember I was just dozing off when Stephen let out a great cry. He had seen a shooting star. He said he made a wish but wouldn't tell me what it was. Now I'll never know.

When morning came we packed our gear in silence. Eventually, miserably, I said, 'Stephen, I don't want to go home.'

'Neither do I.'

We just stood and looked at each other mournfully.

'Do you think they'll know,' I said.

'Know what?'

'About us.'

'Jesus, I hope not!'

'Would it be so terrible?'

'Are you joking? Of course it would be.'

Stephen put down his bedroll and took me by the shoulders. His face was deadly serious. 'Don't you see, Red? If they knew, then they'd never let us be alone together and your father would never trust me again.'

'Oh Stephen, why all this shit about trust? Don't they know we aren't children any more?'

'Honestly, Red, I really do believe they think we still are.'

'Stephen, for heaven's sake . . . '

'Red, your father would never have let you come if he thought we'd sleep together. If you tell him you'll spoil everything.'

In spite of myself, I smiled. 'I wasn't actually going to tell him.' I suddenly saw myself saying, By the way Daddy, Stephen and I had sex while we were away. Aren't we naughty? 'I just thought we'd act as if we were more than just friends, that's all.'

'No!' he said vehemently. 'Please, Rina, it would be a mistake. Don't ask me how I know, I just do. Promise me you'll treat me the same as before?'

'Okay,' I sighed. Giving in. Not really understanding but giving in anyway. 'Whatever you say, boss.'

We hoisted our backpacks and set off. I turned and took one last look at my beloved hills, took one last breath of that clear air. I could hear a buzzard mewing in the distance. It seemed to be saying goodbye.

I thought about what Stephen had said all the way home. It would be hard, not telling anyone, acting like friends, like brother and sister. Stephen was right, of course. My father would hate it if he knew. He still thought of me as his little girl. It seemed such a long time to wait until I was eighteen. Such a great chunk from my life.

I wished then that my mother was alive. I hadn't wished that for ages. If she hadn't died, I'd never have met Stephen, but all the same I wished she'd be there at home. Lots of girls can't talk to their mothers but I would have been able to, I know. Blun told me my mother was a lively, beautiful woman able to break down the barriers of my father's inhibitions – something I'd never really been able to do.

There would be Blun, of course. Dear, sweet Blun. She would understand. Or would she? I felt so confused. And what about Jean? She'd never understand. She'd hate to think I was taking her precious Stephen away from her. Her love for him was so total she would imagine there was no room for anyone else. Such plans for him – university, some boring career – she'd never understand!

I sighed and put my hand on Stephen's leg. He took my fingers and played with them absent-mindedly.

'You're quiet for a change,' he said. 'What are you thinking about?'

'Just how hard it will be to treat you like a brother.'

'I'll be back at school soon and you won't be able to treat me as anything.'

'I don't think I can bear it.'

He squeezed my fingers. 'You'll be okay.'

'I shan't. I shall grow pale and gaunt like Isolde and gradually fade away.'

He laughed. 'Not you – you're too strong for that.'

'How do you know I'm strong?'

'You're always trying to prove it.'

I punched him. 'Cheeky pig.'

He took his eyes off the road for a split second

and looked at me. 'You *are* strong, you know, Red. It's because you are that your father doesn't think you need him.'

'What?'

'It's why he pretends not to care all that much about you – you are so self-sufficient and he isn't.'

I shrugged. 'He just doesn't like expressing his feelings, that's all.'

'It's because he thinks you don't need him to.'

'I do need him to, Stephen.' Stupid of me but I felt like crying.

'I know that, love.'

I put my cheek against his shoulder. 'I need you.'

'I need you too.'

I began to cry. Stephen stopped the car in a lay-by and held me while I sobbed. I don't really know why I cried – I suppose it was for all the lonely years. For my father. For me. For finding Stephen. For having someone to hold at last.

Only Jean was there when we got home. My father had taken Aunt Jo to the hospital. She still hadn't recovered from the 'flu and had been sent to see a specialist.

Jean hugged and kissed Stephen and admired his tan. I grinned to myself thinking how shocked she'd be if she knew it was one of those 'all over' tans. She hugged me too. I think she was as pleased to see me as she was to see her son. I wondered if her eyes might search me for signs of lost virginity but they didn't.

'Rina, you look wonderful,' she said. 'So healthy

– all that exercise has done you good.' Stephen and I exchanged glances over her head. 'Have you had a good time?'

We went indoors, the three of us – Jean in the middle, an arm round us both. I felt then I almost loved her. After all she was Stephen's mother, wasn't she?

'Where's Blun?' I dumped my bag on the kitchen floor. I'd hoped she'd be here to greet us too.

'Rina, dear,' Jean went to put the kettle on. 'I've told her she need not come so often now – her rheumatism is so bad, she really can't cope with standing for long periods of time.'

I whirled, scared. 'You haven't said she needn't come at all?'

'No, of course not,' Jean soothed. 'She asked me if she could do less hours – it's completely her own decision.'

I frowned, not trusting her. 'Are you sure?'

'Yes. I said you'd go and see her tomorrow and tell her about the holiday.'

I sighed with relief. If Jean had told her she wasn't needed any more I'd never forgive her. I couldn't do without Blun. Not ever.

Over the first decent cup of tea we'd had for a week Jean told us Aunt Jo was very ill. She had got worse and was coughing up blood. The doctor had been several times. I felt a stab of fear.

'What do you think is wrong with her?'

Jean shook her head. 'I don't know, Rina. I'm afraid to think about it.'

I didn't like Jean being afraid, as if what might be wrong with Jo was too awful to contemplate.

'How's Daddy?' I said.

'He's fine. He's missed you both.'

'I bet he *hasn't* missed me.'

Jean laughed. 'Now you know that's not true.'

'Don't take any notice of her,' Stephen said. 'She just says that sort of thing so we'll tell her how wonderful she is.'

'Liar!'

Stephen put his arms over his head to protect himself.

I went and bashed him anyway.

Jean smiled benevolently at her two children.

'I can see you two have come back the best of friends,' she said.

And we were the best of friends, the best of lovers too. I wondered again what on earth Jean would say if she knew.

Chapter Eleven

We learned later just how ill my Aunt Jo was.

We were watching TV when we heard them come in. I went out to say hello but Jean was already helping Jo make her slow, painful way to her room. I heard Jean murmuring words of comfort.

My father came into the front room. He looked tired – ill himself. He ruffled my hair and shook Stephen's hand.

'Did you have a good time?'

We told him we had, but somehow our holiday seemed marred by Jo's illness.

My father looked me up and down and seemed satisfied with what he saw. Then he sat down with a sigh and told us about Aunt Jo.

She had to go to hospital. She had cancer. The word struck terror into us all. I thought of all those empty cigarette packets she left lying around the place, the smell of smoke always about her clothes. I thought of her messing about in the kitchen with her bird cakes. I began to cry.

My father looked helpless, not knowing how to comfort me. He came and patted my shoulder awkwardly.

'Don't cry, Rina,' he said. I never know why people say that. What else could I do? Stephen's face was mournful. He knew how to comfort me but didn't dare.

I took Aunt Jo up the present we'd bought. It was only a Welsh dragon made of scarlet felt. It seemed ridiculous to give it to her. What could you give to someone who was going to die?

She lay on the bed like a restless ghost. Pale, turning now and then as if trying to ease the pain. She was awkwardly propped up on half a dozen pillows but she seemed not to have the strength to make herself comfy. Her breath was like a file going to and fro on a piece of wood. Even though it was only a week since I'd seen her, the change in her face was like a hundred years.

It was dark in the room. 'Can I draw back the curtains? Will it hurt your eyes?' I thought it was probably too late to try to be nice to her but I was so full of guilt it was like a knife in my stomach.

'Yes – just a little bit,' she wheezed, trying to sit up higher. I helped her, rearranging the pillows to support her back. She looked pale and dry as a leaf in autumn.

'We bought you this.' I handed her the pathetic parcel. I felt like crying again but my father said we must try and act normally. From the shelf the pictures of her lover stared at me accusingly as if it was all my fault. The picture of Stephen caught my eye. Aunt Jo wearily undid the tissue paper. It seemed as if even that was too much effort.

'Thank you, Katharine,' she said, looking at it

with a slightly puzzled expression on her face. 'It's lovely. Did you have a nice time?'

'Yes – it was really great.'

'Where did you go?'

I told her.

'I went to Wales several times when I was young,' she croaked, her voice dreamy, far away. Then she stopped and looked at me. Her eyes had sunk into her head as if they were trying to escape. 'Rina.' She tried to put the dragon on the bedside table, each movement an effort. I took it from her and propped it up against the lamp. 'There's something I must tell you.' She stopped, a fit of coughing interrupting her sentence. I got off the bed, frightened and embarrassed and helpless. She really didn't have to tell me about her lover now – it could wait, it really could. To my relief Jean came in.

'I think you'd better tell her about the holiday later,' she said, drawing the curtains together again and helping Jo hold a handkerchief to her mouth. I just stood there like a statue until Jo had finished her fit of coughing and collapsed against the pillows, grey with exhaustion. Jean fussed about, drawing the blankets over her.

I crept out. Sad. Forgotten.

In the car, going to visit Blun, I cried again. Stephen stopped and put his arm around me. He had the sense at least not to tell me not to cry. He just held me while I sobbed out my remorse on his shoulder.

'I can't bear it,' I sobbed. 'I've been so beastly to her and now she's dying.'

He kissed my wet face. 'You haven't been beastly to her. She understands what kind of person you are – you have been her whole life, you and John. You've got absolutely nothing to feel guilty about.'

'She was going to tell me about her sweetheart and now she never will.'

'Maybe she will – we can visit her in hospital. John says she has a few months yet.'

'What's a few months when I've got nearly seventeen years of indifference to make up for?'

'But you love the old girl, you told me.'

I looked up into his face. 'I know, but I never told *her* that.'

'Oh Red.' His face looked so regretful it was almost comical. I thought how grown-up he looked, how mature. He'd changed quite a bit since the photo was taken – the one of him in Aunt Jo's room.

I half managed a smile and Stephen gave me his hanky to blow my nose. It smelt of oil where he had been fiddling with the car. I felt a bit better and made up my mind I would tell Aunt Jo I loved her before she died.

But Aunt Jo didn't have a few months. She only had a few weeks. There was a dark shadow over those weeks – the dark shadow of death.

They took Aunt Jo to a hospice where people go to die. They had given her some treatment but it was no good. It was already too late.

We went each day to see her. By her bed was a photograph of her sweetheart.

The room she was in was warm and softly lit. Nurses moved around quietly like shadows. I sat and held her hand. Although she was sedated she knew I was there.

'Tell me about your friend now, Aunt Jo,' I whispered, not really knowing if she could hear me or not.

'His name was Albert,' she said in a voice surprisingly loud.

'Did you love him very much?'

'Very much.' Her hand moved restlessly in mine as if she was trying to reach out for the past. From the other side of the room Stephen watched. The whole place seemed to be filled with Jo's painful breathing. Spirits of death flitted in corners. She smiled at me. 'You know, Katharine,' she whispered, 'your father was only a baby when our parents were killed – he was more like my own child than a brother. And you – together you healed the wound.'

'I'm glad,' I said. Then, leaning close, I whispered. 'I love you, Aunt Jo.'

She smiled again and squeezed my hand. Then she closed her eyes. I rested my forehead on the back of her hand. I felt Stephen's fingers on my shoulder.

'Come on, Red – she's gone to sleep.'

* * *

When things got worse my father wouldn't let us visit her. He stayed home from the office and went every day. Jean stayed home too. I wanted desperately to see Aunt Jo and pleaded with them to let me go. My father was adamant.

'There's no point,' he said. 'She doesn't know anyone now and I'd rather you remembered her as she was.'

But he and Jean kept going just the same.

The house was silent – a kind of miasma of sadness lay over it. I imagined I could hear the swish of Aunt Jo's long skirts coming down the stairs; the clink of spoons from the kitchen as she made her smelly cakes. The door of her room was closed tight, like the entrance to a tomb.

Stephen and I, left on our own, spent some time sorting out his things for school. His departure was looming over us too. Two shadows – death and departure. I didn't know if I could bear it.

When we could no longer stand it indoors we went down to the summerhouse. It had been our sanctuary all summer long. We had been painting the outside and it was almost finished. Neither of us felt like doing it now.

Inside, our collection of drawings were pinned to the back wall, some photographs we'd taken; stuff we'd collected on holiday was there too. Fossils, the sloughed skin of an adder, some pressed flowers. Reminders. In the drawer of the old chest, locked, were our private drawings. Some of Stephen, some of me naked on a rock by the pool. Notes we'd written, some poems. We both had a key.

We lay together on the old settee. Just holding tight. Thinking about Aunt Jo, thinking about Stephen going back to school. I wished we could stay there for ever, close like that. I wished our lives could have stopped there.

Aunt Jo died that night. I didn't cry when I heard. I didn't think then that I had any tears left.

I did though.

I had plenty.

I didn't even cry at Aunt Jo's funeral. She hadn't wanted any flowers but I took a rose from her beloved garden and laid it on her coffin. A funeral without flowers is like winter without snow.

Lots of people came back to the house afterwards. A few friends of my father's who knew Aunt Jo from their visits to our house. People from the village who had known her for so many years. The shopkeeper, ladies from the WI. I bet they'd miss her at their jumble sales. People I hardly knew at all. I couldn't bear listening to everyone talking so loudly over their glasses of sherry. I hate funerals. I hate funeral parties even more. It was hard to believe Aunt Jo was really dead until I saw that coffin disappearing and the curtains closing. It was like the end of some ghastly stage show.

I felt sorry for the birds – they were going to have a really lean time of it without cakes to gorge themselves on.

I sneaked out and went down to the stream. I took out the black ribbon that held back my hair and shook it free. In the distance I could hear the roar of the combine harvester. I thought of all the little creatures it was killing as it went along. Clouds of dust rose like smoke. Soon the plough would come and the earth would be brown again. Then green; another season beginning. I thought about Aunt Jo – she loved the autumn, bright colours all around. I wondered if she had ever made love to Albert. I wondered if she had ever known what it was like – the touch of lips on hers, of skin, a breathed name in her ear. I wondered what it was she so desperately wanted to tell me when all I'd ever learned was Albert's name. Now I'd never know.

Stephen came and sat beside me. He put his hand on my shoulder.

'You okay, Red? Been crying?'

I smiled at him wanly. 'No, I just couldn't stand listening to all those hypocrites. None of them really cared about her.'

'How do you know?'

I shrugged and turned away. 'I just know. Anyway she didn't care about them. She only cared about Albert.'

'And you and John.'

'Yes.' I turned to him and took his hand in my own. It was big and brown and had paint spots on the back. I held it to my cheek. 'And you – there's a picture of you in her room.'

'My mother must have given it to her.'

'Yes.'

'Poor old Jo.'

We sat in silence, gazing out over the meadow. I was glad I'd told her I loved her. I wonder if she knew all along? I wonder if she really loved me or whether she just said that about me helping her get over Albert because she was dying. I suppose she must have loved me really or she wouldn't have put up with me all those years.

I put my head on Stephen's shoulder. He put his arm round me. He was usually scared to do that in case someone saw.

Chapter Twelve

Soon after that Stephen went back to school. I couldn't even kiss him goodbye. Not properly anyway. It was my first day at college and he had taken me to the station before setting off.

'See you at Christmas,' he said.

But he didn't.

My father asked Jean and me if we would sort out Aunt Jo's things. It wasn't a man's job, he said. I didn't see why not but couldn't be bothered to argue. That shows I was depressed.

A few evenings later I crept up to Aunt Jo's room, alone. It didn't seem right for Jean to touch her things – she wasn't really a relation. On my way up the telephone rang. I ran back down.

It was Stephen.

'How are you, Red?'

'Fine,' I lied. How could I tell him the truth with Jean and my father listening from the kitchen.

'How's college?'

'All right – how's school?'

'Bloody awful – I miss you.'

'Me too.' I wanted to say 'I love you' but Jean was breathing down my neck. I gave her the phone and went back upstairs. My legs felt heavy as if my heart had sunk right down to my shoes.

Jo's room smelt funny – different. I suppose it was because she wasn't there any more. I opened the window to let in some fresh air. The night smelt of bonfires and autumn. I drew the curtains across and put on the light.

The pictures of Albert were gone, and the one of Stephen. I wondered who had taken it. I wouldn't have minded it for the shelf in my room.

The wardrobe door was open. All Jo's crazy dresses hung there like dead flowers. The floaty, floral things she loved. Things she had thought made her look young. I ran my hand along them – her smell crept out.

On the shelf were hats – straw for summer, felt for winter. Some knitted ones she got at junk sales. Aunt Jo was never without a hat. I took a wide-brimmed black one and plonked it on my head. I stood in front of the mirror, frowning. I screwed up my face and the feather in the hat fell over one eye. I decided I'd look like Jo when I was old. Maybe I'd be as crazy too. I put the hat back in the wardrobe and shut the door. I felt guilty, like an intruder. She'd hate me being there if she knew. Maybe she did know. I didn't believe in ghosts or the afterlife or anything but I had an uncanny feeling Jo was still in that room. So much of her was still here – maybe the spirit of her was inextricably tied up in these things she had left behind?

Someone had stacked all the paintings against one wall. I knew my father had given some to her friends and Stephen had asked if he could take one back to school with him. It was one of me when I was small – scruffy red hair like a bush all round my freckled face. It had made him laugh. I imagined it now hanging in his room. Everyone asking who it was and why the hell he'd hung it there. I wished I was there in his room instead of here in Aunt Jo's – alone but for the remnants of a sad and lonely life.

Stupidly I began to cry. I always seemed to be doing that lately. Jean came in.

'Rina!' She put her arm round me and sat with me on the bed. Someone had stripped it and the bare mattress felt cold, unyielding.

Jean just sat there while I cried. Being near to her was like being near to Stephen – or part of him anyway. I suppose she thought I was crying for Jo.

I felt better after a bit, sniffed and fished a tissue from the pocket of my jeans. I felt a bit silly.

'I was going to ask you if you wanted to sort some of your aunt's things out,' she said, 'but it doesn't look as if you feel much like it at the moment.'

'Do you mind?'

She smiled her eternally patient smile. 'Of course not – we'll do it some other time. It is an awful thing but it has to be done.'

'Have you had to do it before?' I realised suddenly I knew nothing about Jean – her past, her family.

'Yes, my father, then my mother – and several friends have asked me to help them before now.'

'Stephen's grandparents?'

102

'Yes.'

I wondered then about Stephen's father and wanted to ask her but didn't dare. If she wouldn't tell him then I didn't expect for one minute she'd tell me. I wondered if she'd had other lovers. People didn't have so many in those days – or that's what they would have you believe.

We stood up and Jean walked with me to the door. 'We'll do some sorting out at the weekend . . . if you feel up to it – if you feel better.'

'Yes,' I said.

But I didn't.

I stayed in my room for a while. Listening to old Rod, looking through the photos of our summer holiday, reading some poetry. I missed Stephen so much.

Later Jean came in with a cup of coffee. She put it on the bedside table and handed me an envelope. It had my name on.

'I found this,' she said, 'inside Jo's book of poetry. She must have meant to give it to you before she went to the hospice.'

I thought of other notes Jo had written me. Often she would leave one which read, 'Dinner in the oven', and when I looked there was nothing in there. Or 'Gone shopping' and she would come back empty-handed, her attention diverted by something else entirely.

'Thanks,' I said and took it from her as if it was just another of Aunt Jo's crazy notes. As if it didn't contain news of the end of the world.

I looked at the envelope for a while after Jean had gone. It seemed weird, getting a note from someone who was dead. I held it up to the light, you know, the way you do, trying to see what it says inside as if it would be clever of you to guess what it was.

In a million years I would never have guessed what this one said.

The first thing that fell out was a photograph. The one of Stephen in cricket clothes. I felt pleased she had left it for me, she must have known I liked it. I hadn't seen it really close before and now I noticed there was something odd about it.

First of all it was old – yellowed round the edges as if it had been handled a lot and warped where it had stood in the sun. And his cricket gear was funny – old-fashioned, his hair cut really short like a schoolboy thirty years ago. Maybe it was for a fancy dress, I thought, puzzled.

How stupid I was. How ignorant, how blind.

Just then a cold gust of wind blew into the room, billowing out the curtains and blowing a piece of paper off my desk. I put Aunt Jo's envelope and photograph on the bed and went to shut the window. I picked the paper up off the floor. It was the beginning of a letter I had been writing to Stephen.

As I stood by the window a cloud scudded across the moon. I shivered and got a cardigan from the drawer. Then I sat back on the bed and began to read Aunt Jo's letter.

Chapter Thirteen

It's still hard to think about Jo's letter. Lots of things are hard to think about – that's the hardest of all.

I remember sitting on the bed and picking up the photograph again, holding it in one hand, the letter in the other. I remember turning the picture over – 'John Mortimer' it said on the back, 'Upper VI'. That's daft, I thought, who put my father's name on the back of a picture of Stephen?

When I read the letter I knew.

'My dear Katharine' – it seemed funny to see my name written like that; I even sign myself 'Rina' –

I wanted to tell you this before Jean and John got married but they said you were both so young that you probably wouldn't understand and that you were to get to know each other first and accept the new family situation before they told you. John said he could not think of a suitable way of telling you without you feeling betrayed. But when I think of myself and Albert – how we loved each other when we were hardly older than you, Katharine, and dear Stephen – I know we understood many things, things our parents would never have imagined.

So she *did* make love to him, I thought stupidly, still not realising what the letter was trying to tell me.

> And seeing you and Stephen together, seeing the way your friendship is developing I know that someone must tell you soon. You see, my dear Katharine . . .

Here the writing tailed off with a smudge of ink. I guessed poor Aunt Jo must have been overtaken by a fit of coughing. Then she started again:

> Stephen is your brother – your true half-brother. Your father and Jean knew one another many years ago before he married your mother. He and Jean were lovers. Then they quarrelled and parted, your father never knowing Jean was carrying his child. He met your mother very soon afterwards and they were married within weeks. I felt I must tell you this before it was too late.

But it *is* too late, dear, crazy Aunt Jo.

> Please do not think too badly of your father for not telling you, Katharine. He does not want you to know he behaved badly all those years ago. He feels so guilty about leaving Jean alone to bring up Stephen. Now he has made up for that – now he has Jean and Stephen and you, all together, his family. Dear Rina,

do not be broken-hearted. Do not live a life of mourning. It is an empty life. Stephen is a wonderful young man – a brother is a great gift. I know. Without your father I could not have recovered from the loss of Albert.

The letter was signed 'Josephine'.

She was crazier than I thought. Really crazy – making up stories. Maybe she was getting her own back for all the times I'd been horrible to her. Maybe it was some awful, sick joke – the imaginings of a tortured mind.

I read the letter three times. Only then did it really begin to sink in. Then I looked at the photograph once more and the bottom fell out of my world. My hand shook so much I could hardly see it. It was like looking through a thick and terrible fog.

Of course, it wasn't Stephen at all. It was my father as a boy. How stupid I was not to have noticed before. Aunt Jo wasn't crazy at all – what she was telling me was the truth. How could I have been so blind not to see the likeness. My father – a mirror image of Stephen – his son.

For a while I couldn't move. I just sat there, letter in one hand, photograph in the other. Gradually, horribly I screwed the picture up, tight, into a ball. It seemed as if a great weight had fallen from the sky and was crushing me to bits. I stared at the floor expecting to see pieces of myself scattered all around.

I suppose I began to cry then. Quietly at first –

the kind of crying you do when someone has died. Then louder until I knew I was hysterical. It was strange, knowing that. Knowing you are screaming and sobbing but not being able to do anything about it. As if you have left your body and are watching it from some other place. Knowing it's you but not being able to control what you are doing.

I heard a knocking at the door, worried voices calling my name. I couldn't answer because my mind was filled with that dreadful noise that somehow seemed to be coming from me.

Chapter Fourteen

Blun told me afterwards I *had* been hysterical. They had to send for a doctor. He gave me an injection of something to shut me up. I didn't know what it was. I didn't care a lot. He left me some pills too but I wouldn't take them. Even on the very bad days when the ghosts were all around I knew I had to try to get over it on my own.

The Grey person, and my father, tried to fuss over me all the time. But I ignored the tears in their eyes. The faces full of remorse. I didn't care that they suffered too. I didn't care that they crept around like strangers, avoiding each other's eyes, avoiding contact, as if they both had something catching.

The only person I would speak to was Blun. She was my rock – my salvation. I knew I'd have to speak to Jean and my father again one day. Silence kills. I didn't think I could go on hating them for ever.

They wouldn't let Stephen come to see me. They said it was better for us not to see each other for a while.

I didn't know what good they thought that would do. Did they think it would stop us loving each other? They said that we would get over it, that we were young. Why do people always think the young recover easily?

Then – late one night – he did come. It had taken him ages to get here – driving up from school after lessons had finished. My father and Jean were both asleep. Blun let him in. She had been staying at the house for a few days.

I was still awake. I didn't sleep much anyway. I was lying there looking at the moon through the gap in the curtains. I was remembering how I told Stephen I used to think you could catch it. Then, suddenly, the door opened softly and he was there. Just for a moment I thought you *could* catch the dream in your hands after all – even if you did have to let it go again.

We just held each other all night. For a while we couldn't even speak. Eventually we talked. And cried. We didn't solve anything – there was no way of ever doing that.

'Why can't we just go away and live together?' I sobbed. 'No one would know.' I didn't care that he was my brother.

'That wouldn't be fair to you, Red,' he said, his voice cracking as if it was as broken as his heart. 'You could never have children.'

'I don't care. I don't care.'

But I knew he was right. We couldn't live a lie for the rest of our lives. It was lies and deceit that had destroyed us in the first place.

'What I can't understand,' Stephen said, running his hands through his hair, 'is *why* they thought they were doing the right thing? They must be absolutely mad, both of them.'

I shook my head. 'I don't know, I don't know.'

How many hearts have been broken, I wondered, how many lives ruined because people insist on doing what they believe to be the right thing?

Then he kissed me and crept away. I heard the mini roaring away down the lane, taking with it my life, my soul, taking the musician that played symphonies with my heart.

I did a stupid thing after that. I tried to kill myself. It seemed, at the time, the only thing to do.

Mr Blun found me in the summerhouse. I remember thinking, through a red haze of pain, that he'd probably have a heart attack running up the garden like that, running like a crazy man with news of the end of the world.

They let Stephen come to see me in hospital. He looked awful. He had bags under his eyes, his face was haunted. He held my bandaged wrists to his lips. We both cried a lot and he made me promise never to try to kill myself again. I said I never would. It had been a stupid thing to do anyway. He said we didn't have to stop loving each other, nothing could ever stop us doing that. We just could never be together the way we wanted, that was all. He told me he was leaving school and going to Australia for a year. A friend of his had an uncle with a sheep farm – he was going to work there.

111

'What about your A-levels?' I said. 'What about your mother?'

He shrugged. 'I'll do them at college when I come back. And I don't care about my mother. She's betrayed me, Rina – lied to me. Why the hell should I care *what* she wants?'

He told me then that I must be strong. It was only by me being strong that he would survive too. He said I must remember that when he'd gone. He made me promise. I did. It's awful when someone tells you you've got to be strong. You feel such a failure when you turn out to be weak like everybody else.

He left me then.

I haven't seen him since.

I think of him now. A million miles away, his face bronzed under the Australian sun, hair bleached blonder than ever. I wonder if there are any girls there? Girls like the one in the village near his old school. Girls he doesn't love.

In October a year will have passed since Stephen went away. Now I know I can think of him without pain. Only the joyful memories of that summer survive and the jagged edges of the wound have almost healed. I suppose if there's one thing I have learned it's that we can't always have the things we most want. Things we believe we cannot live without. At least to have had them for a while is better than never knowing.

The summerhouse is where I write.

During the winter they cleaned it up. The blood wouldn't come off the sofa so they burned it and bought a new one. The chest is still here though – the one with our things locked up inside. One day maybe I'll have the courage to open it.

I turn my wrists – the scars are still there, memories stitched in flesh. Sewn forever into my skin.

Old Rod's here, keeping me company, rasping away as usual – 'still I'd look to find a reason to believe . . . ' That's what I've been looking for, I suppose, all the long dark winter of my grief – a reason to believe.

Outside the sun still shines. Birds still sing – tumbling notes in the fragrant summer evening. Mr Blundell cut the grass today and the smell wafts its memories towards me.

Stephen will be back soon. I hope I'll feel completely sane by then. I might even have filled my life – other friendships, another love.

Or maybe I'll end up being just a little crazy like Aunt Jo.